MOCHA MAYHEM

THE COZY CAFÉ MYSTERIES

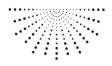

C. A. PHIPPS

For my wonderful Beta Readers
Thank you for all your hard work, Suzanne and Bernie.
You are awesome! x

MOCHA MAYHEM

A seaside wedding.

The perfect catering job for The Cozy Café.

Except for the body!

Wanting to put the café firmly on the map, Scarlett
didn't imagine things would go so horribly wrong when she
took a wedding job at the last minute.

Along with her sisters, she's once more embroiled in a case
where people aren't who they say and murder appears to be
an inconvenience.
Sadly, when money has too much power, families are in
turmoil, and a close friend hides their feelings so well, Scarlett has no idea how to untangle this web.

Even the sheriff is struggling to get people to talk and
knowing that the culprit is in their midst makes things
decidedly uncomfortable.

Meanwhile, George the cat is unimpressed to have a visitor in the house and he's quite happy to let everyone know about it!

The Cozy Café mysteries are light, cozy mysteries featuring a family-focused café owner who discovers she's a talented amateur sleuth—and a magnet for animals.

No swearing, gore, or graphic scenes.

The Cozy Café Series:
Book 1 Sweet Saboteur
Book 2 Candy Corruption
Book 3 Mocha Mayhem
Enjoy a FREE sweet treat recipe in every book.

5* "The sheriff and Scarlett have their handles full trying to unravel this mystery. I could not put it down." by Bernadette Cinkoske

Please sign up for my new release mailing list and pick up a free recipe book!

CHAPTER ONE

Scarlett's anxiety spiked as a second sugar rose slipped from her fingers to smash into fragments on the tiled floor. This cake had taken three days to make, and if she didn't fix her mistake ASAP, the bride wouldn't be cutting anything that looked halfway decent.

Her hometown of Cozy Hollow might not be at the forefront of sophistication. Still, twenty miles inland and north of Harmony Beach, it had everything a person needed and good old-fashioned manners in bucket loads.

Here at Harmony Beach, things were a little different. People had money and liked everyone else to know about it. The Turners were no exception. Nothing was too good for their little girl, Lexie. If the original company they'd hired to cater for the event hadn't pulled out, Scarlett and her sisters wouldn't have had the opportunity to help with the food or make the cake. This fact was pointed out many times.

Positive feedback from catering for the prestigious Turner/Wood wedding would undoubtedly put The Cozy Café on the map, so Scarlett took the digs at her ability with as much good grace as she could muster. Her café was her passion, and therefore she could handle being talked down to for one more day.

While she managed not to drop the next rose, the family chef came into his massive pantry to check on things as he'd done repeatedly since Scarlett and her two sisters arrived that morning.

"Aren't you finished with that yet?"

"Just about, Chef. Do you like it?"

He looked down his nose and walked around the table. "It's acceptable."

Really? Scarlett bit her tongue to keep from telling him a thing or two he wouldn't like to hear, but stopped quickly, as it hurt!

"Just give me a few more minutes to add the finishing touches."

He stalked out as if he wanted to give her something else, which wasn't likely to be praise. Taking a deep breath and forcing herself to concentrate on the cake rather than the hundred other things that needed doing, Scarlett managed to get the last roses in place. She stood back and wiped her hands as someone else came through the door.

"That looks fantastic! And you look pretty cute, with that icing on your cheek."

Sam Drake was the paramedic based in Cozy Hollow, and she was pleased to see him. Grinning, she wiped the offending mess with a corner of her starched white apron. "You don't look so shabby yourself."

"I'll take that." Sam preened, pulling at his waistcoat, which was very snug.

"Since you're his best man, shouldn't you be with the groom?"

Sam shrugged. "Chad's got his brother there. They're having a moment."

"And you don't do moments?" she teased.

"I wouldn't say that." Sam came closer and took her hands. "I'm still hoping for a moment or two with you."

She shook her hands free. "Shhh. Not here. I'm working, unlike you."

"One day, there will be a right time. Maybe after you've finished for the evening, we could meet up for a bit?"

He looked a little desperate, and Scarlett was flattered. Dating for a few months, they found it hard to factor in time together when Scarlett lived with her sisters, and Sam always seemed to be working or on call.

"It's going to be a long day in the kitchen, and you've got your best man duties. They may last quite a while longer than the food."

He frowned. "A man could be forgiven for thinking you'd changed your mind about dating me."

"That man would be silly. I haven't," she promised, leaning in to kiss his cheek. He turned quickly and snuck a peck on the lips. "Sam!"

"What? I'm a paramedic. It's my job to check that you're breathing okay."

Scarlett snorted. Her heart had already done several twirls at the sight of him in his navy suit and tie. Add the crisp white shirt and paisley waistcoat—Sam was definitely swoon-worthy. Still, as much as she enjoyed it, she wouldn't be able to concentrate if he was going to flirt with her all night.

"When you lovebirds are done, can you check the tables, Scarlett?" Olivia Greene stood in the doorway, a broad smile on her face.

Asked to do the wedding a few weeks ago, they'd also roped in their mom's sister to help.

"I'll be there in a minute. Sam's helping me put the cake somewhere safe."

Scarlett's youngest sister, Ruby, peered over Olivia's shoulder and giggled. "Sure, that's the only reason he's here."

A tall woman came up behind Ruby, towering over her. Since Ruby was rather short, this wasn't hard.

"I trust everything is going to plan?" Mrs. Turner was a perfectionist and very loud about it.

Poor Ruby jumped, while Scarlett somehow managed to keep a straight face.

"It is." With a surprisingly steady hand, considering her audience, she slipped the last few flowers into place with a flourish. "The cake's finished. Now I just need a place to put it."

Mrs. Turner pointed behind her. "There's the kitchen office in the opposite corner. Chef won't mind."

Scarlett imagined that it was too bad if he did because Mrs. Turner had spoken, and she hadn't seen one person attempt to disagree with the woman. The others moved back into the kitchen to let Scarlett and Sam pass, carefully wheeling the cake into the office. Scarlett noticed a door to the outside. This would make getting it into the large tent easier than through the kitchen doors, which the waiters would be using.

When they returned, Mrs. Turner glared at them as though they had dawdled.

"The guests will be arriving any minute. Are the tables set?"

Scarlett nodded. "Yes. And your chef and I have the food organized. We'll bring out the canapés whenever you like."

"Just have them ready. My staff will do the waiting. As I've explained, they're the professionals. Sam, I'm sure that Chad needs your services."

"Sure, thing. I'll be on my way back to Chad once I've checked on the groomsman."

Seemingly unfazed by the command, Sam weathered the

down-the-nose glare expertly. Scarlett also noticed that the chef kept himself busy with the roast meats he was cooking and didn't join the conversation. Not that she blamed him. In the short time, she'd known Mrs. Turner, Scarlett could appreciate that the less said, the better the outcome.

An extended counter ran down the kitchen's length, narrowing the walkway, but necessary for when it came time to set up the entrée, mains, and then dessert.

"Good luck, and I'll see you later," Sam waved as he followed Chad's mother-in-law to be down the hall leading to the central part of the house.

Scarlett joined Olivia and Ruby in the main tent, where Violet made last-minute adjustments to the cutlery and checked glassware.

"Top job, Vi. The settings look the same as the diagram we were given."

"Thank goodness. Mrs. Turner's been through here countless times and has always found something to fix." Violet rolled her eyes.

Scarlett shrugged. "Well, she's paying for it. I guess she has a right."

'Hah! As if anyone checks that their knife and fork is so many inches from the end of the table."

"Maybe not in our circles, but it is a thing elsewhere. Obviously, this is *elsewhere*," Scarlett teased.

Her sister had no comeback, which was rare.

"Since it's all done in here, can everyone help me lay out the canapes on trays, please? I'm not sure where we'll find room to put them, but hopefully, they'll go out as soon as we plate them."

"Of course." Olivia had been on her feet for as long as the girls and her stamina hadn't waned. In her fifties, she seemed excited by the day and didn't struggle with any job asked of her.

Scarlett was very proud of her family and the way they'd risen to the challenge. It was a huge undertaking, no matter that there was other staff to share the burden. The last caterers undoubtedly had more experience with this kind of function, while she, her aunt and sisters, had none.

On their way back to the kitchen, Scarlett stopped to address a young waiter. "Tony, could you please check all the lower floor bathrooms to ensure the toilet tissue is plentiful and the baskets with hand towels are full?"

Unsure why Mrs. Turner thought this sort of management was part of the caterer's job; she suspected the woman had lost even more staff recently. Scarlett was pretty sure she knew the reason why.

He saluted with a cheeky twinkle in his eye. "At once, ma'am."

As he raced off, a couple arrived at the tent opening. They took in the interior, then walked toward the flower-draped wedding arch. Seating was arranged in a half-circle facing this and the water. Beyond this was a small dock and steps leading down to the beach.

Scarlett turned to her team. "Quick, they're early, but we still need to offer them refreshments."

They hurried into the kitchen, where another waiter was opening wine.

"Leo, some guests have arrived. They're out by the arch."

"I'll attend to them now," he said stiffly.

As the head waiter, he didn't appreciate any suggestions Scarlett made and didn't bother to hide it, unlike the chef who was somewhat grateful for their help and appeared to be trying not to resent them too much.

"Perfect. We'll bring some canapés out for your team to hand out shortly."

Nose in the air, Leo draped a white cloth carefully over

6

his arm and took a tray of half-filled glasses of champagne and wine outside.

Scarlett refused to let him bother her. It wasn't her fault that the caterers pulled out of the wedding, or that no one else would consider helping on such short notice. Leo and his staff should be grateful and want to work together. If they didn't, Mrs. Turner would have something to say.

Finding the designated trays in the large pantry, while her sisters and aunt took out containers from the walk-in refrigerator, they placed small blini with cream fraise, salmon, and a sprig of dill on each tray. After a touch of seasoning, she added tiny pastries with feta, salsa, and beetroot. Small meatballs on cocktail sticks and shrimps on crostini plus two small pots of her special sauces filled the last spaces. Lastly, she garnished them with parsley and edible flowers.

"I'll take the first one out to show Mrs. Turner. Can you make more of the same?"

The others nodded, and Scarlett went into the house, carefully balancing the tray, so nothing moved.

Raised voices came from the sitting room where Scarlett's interview was conducted. She hesitated. Should she interrupt or simply take the tray out to a waiter without asking? The wrath of Mrs. Turner could happen in either of these scenarios. Caught between a rock and a hard place, Scarlett straightened her apron and tapped on the door.

Silence. Then there was the clear sound of another door banging.

"Come!" Mrs. Turner's commanding voice rang out.

Scarlett opened the door, not as composed as she might appear. Mrs. Turner sat in an expensive-looking chair that she'd used every time they'd met. Other than the two of them, the room was empty, and the French doors across the room were closed.

"You wanted to see the selection presentation of canapés before they go out."

"Very well. Bring it here, then." The woman snapped her fingers rudely.

Scarlett crossed the thick carpet and bent so that the tray would be easier to view.

"This looks acceptable. Go ahead and serve as soon as anyone arrives."

"A few guests are here already."

Eyes narrowed, Mrs. Turner huffed. "How annoying. Very well. I shall be out there soon."

Scarlett stopped herself from bowing at the clear dismissal, giving a small nod instead. Then she got out of there as fast as she could.

It nagged at her that someone had been in that room, arguing with Mrs. Turner, and she hoped it had nothing to do with her. She shook her head. There was enough to do without worrying about who Mrs. Turner had upset or about what.

CHAPTER TWO

As requested, Scarlett and her team kept out of the way and let the waiters do their thing. Watching from the edge of the tent, they were ready to spring into action when the time came.

With their side of the food preparation done, they wouldn't be required until it was time to serve the cold entree, which entailed dressing the salad and wiping down plates while the chef continued with the main.

Scarlett and her sisters had not only made the wedding cake, they'd also made the desserts. At the interview, she'd taken a selection, including a sample of flavors for the cake. Unable to choose, the bride went with a variety of mini desserts per person and a mocha flavored wedding cake. Mrs. Turner reluctantly agreed, and Scarlett went home elated. Little did she know how taxing the whole event was to be. For one person to have the ability to make so many others miserable was a travesty.

It wasn't as though they were desperate for money anymore. Since having the good fortune to locate a family heirloom, and selling it for a tidy amount, things were finally looking up for them. The problem was that they'd struggled for so long, nearly losing the business their mother had not only built from scratch but had loved so much. Turning down such a lucrative job had proved unthinkable. Hindsight could provide startling clarity.

The wedding was quite simply beautiful.

Three bridesmaids, in pale blue with navy ribbons at their waists, came out of the house first, walking one behind the other with a groomsman beside them. Then came the bride on her father's arm.

There was no flower girl or ring-bearer. Strangely, there were no children at all.

In a gown of ivory silk, Lexie Turner was a fairytale princess. Straps low on her arms cinched in at her tiny waist, it draped around her feet and onto the ground. The train was 15 feet long, and the lace overlay was a piece of art.

The women sighed. Scarlett's sigh may have been louder, because Sam, holding on to his partner's arm, was so handsome. Taking his place next to the groom, looking unnaturally stiff, poor Sam, clearly wasn't comfortable in his three-piece suit. As if to prove a point, he ran a finger around his collar and shot the groom a nervous glance.

Chad, also a fine-looking man, already stood with the celebrant in front of the arch. Nervousness seemed to be the theme of this wedding. Scarlett noted a significant difference with the demeanor of the couple. While the bride had a bright-eyed look of expectation, the groom appeared to be taking no enjoyment from the day.

The father of the bride, a frown also marring his face, handed his daughter to the groom. He seemed about to say something but instead turned abruptly to take his place in the front row next to his wife.

Perhaps the pressure of so many high-profile guests, or the Turner's expectation that everything should be perfect, changed the easy-going groom and best man into these awkward men.

The ceremony took more time than it should due to Chad's struggle to speak his vows, and when it came time, he seemed hard-pressed to say I do. The bride appeared oblivious to the whole thing and kissed her new husband with enthusiasm. On the other hand, with arms locked at his sides, Chad was as stiff as a board. There was no hint of passion from either of them.

"Wow," Violet whispered. "Do you see that? "

"Something's not right," Olivia added quietly.

"He's probably stressed," Ruby said. "Weddings are notorious for that, and I bet he's had a lot to do."

Violet snorted. "He's marrying into the richest family in Harmony Beach, and as we've met the Turners I can't believe he was allowed a say in anything even if he'd wanted to."

"That could be the problem, and maybe Chad wanted to be involved more."

Scarlett smiled at her youngest sister. Ruby always wanted things to be perfect and tried to see only the good in people. "Come on." She pulled on her sister's arms. "We're into phase two."

From that moment, it was a blur. While the couple had photos taken down on the beach, more canapés were taken around. Alcohol flowed freely, and laughter rang around the tent. Without the senior Turners around, the place felt less tense. Even the chef made a few jokes as they worked around him and his team plating the entrees.

As soon as the wedding party returned, these were taken outside to the staff who served the guests so Scarlett's team could move on to plating the main course.

Now they were on the last course, which was a tremendous relief.

"What a wonderful day," Ruby exclaimed from across the

ample steel counter as she placed edible flowers on each plate. "I adore weddings."

"Me too," Aunt Olivia chuckled. "Our worries were unfounded."

"They do seem to be enjoying the day," Scarlett agreed.

Violet shook her head. "Except for the groom who still has a face like a prune."

"Stop it," Scarlett warned her while inspecting each plate for uniformity.

"There's only us here," Violet protested.

Scarlett nodded pointedly at the chef, who was stacking pots and pans for the kitchen staff to deal with later. He didn't react but was definitely close enough to hear.

"Fine." Violet took a laden tray through to the tent, and Scarlett followed with the last of the desserts.

The bride excused herself from a group of people and made her way across the tent to the sisters, waiting until the staff moved off with the trays before she spoke.

"Have you seen Chad?" Lexie's voice was soft yet urgent.

Handing the tray to one of the staff, Scarlett shook her head. "I'm sorry. We've been in the kitchen most of the time."

"Of course, you have." Lexie looked frantically around the tent, muttering, "I don't know what I was thinking."

Scarlett smiled in an attempt to put her at ease since the bride seemed on the point of hysteria. "You look so lovely. That dress is stunning, and the weather's been perfect for your special day."

"Thank you," the bride spoke absently, still searching for someone or something.

"Is everything okay? Can I help you find who you're looking for?"

"I'm probably a little dramatic, but it's time to cut the cake." Lexie hesitated for a moment before continuing. "My mom is not happy that the timing is off, and I've already sent the bridesmaids and groomsmen to look for Chad, with no luck so far."

"Perhaps I could check the washrooms?" Scarlett suggested.

Lexie frowned. "Sam already checked them out."

"Violet and I could help look in other places. We've done all we can for now in here. Maybe no one's looked on the beach?"

Lexie nodded enthusiastically. "Would you mind? That would be so kind. Once the cake's cut, we can get onto the dancing. Then we can leave for our honeymoon."

A certain tightness around Lexie's mouth had Scarlett rethinking that she was oblivious to the groom's behavior. With little experience of weddings, Scarlett thought it was bad-mannered of Chad to force his new bride to search for him, and no doubt, having to make excuses for his disappearance.

"We'll go right now. Don't worry, Lexie, Chad will be around here somewhere."

"Thank you, I do appreciate it. And thank you so much for your part in making this a wonderful experience." Lexie's smile faltered, and she hurried back to the bridal table.

Scarlett motioned Violet to follow her, waiting until they'd gone through the tent and reached the dock, before telling her sister about searching for the groom. Her immediate reaction was grating.

"I bet he's run off with a bridesmaid."

"Violet!"

"Well, that's what usually happens when the groom disappears. Plus, you have to admit that he looked like he was marrying under sufferance."

"Okay, he didn't look happy, but that doesn't mean he wanted to run off. We're not in a soap opera."

Violet shrugged. "Fine. Where shall we look?"

Scarlett did a 360 slow turn from the sea around the expansive back lawn and back. "Well, he's not around here. I suggested we try down on the beach?" "Fine with me. The fresh air will be nice. It was hot in the kitchen and the tent—even with fans going."

"We're still on the clock," Scarlett reminded her as they walked down several wide steps.

"You're such a stickler. They've had their pound of flesh and more, and this is hardly in our job description."

"Maybe not, but potentially we could get a lot of work from this wedding if we do a good job, and more importantly, create the right impression."

"We've done a good job. A great job, actually. Better than the people who pulled out at the last minute, who knew it was going to be a nightmare dealing with Mrs. Davina Turner."

Scarlett shook her head. "Stop trying to wind me up. Customers are still customers."

"Me?"

Scarlett nudged her as they reached the beach, and when Violet giggled, she appreciated, not for the first time, that sisters were a joy and a pain.

They came to a dinghy half-way along the private part of the beach that belonged to the Turners. Whether they owned it or not was another story, but they certainly put it around and acted as though they did.

"I think this is far enough." Scarlett stopped by the boat. "I wonder why it's here."

Violet shrugged. "They probably didn't want it spoiling the view from the tent down to the water and moved it from the dock."

"That makes sense. I can't imagine Chad came this far, though. Why would he when he was supposed to cut the cake? And how would he walk along this beach without someone noticing?" Sun bounced off the sand, and Scarlett shielded her eyes with her hand. "Actually you can't see more than the top of the tent from here."

"He had that trapped look the whole afternoon. Maybe he's run away. Brides aren't the only ones to do that."

This time Scarlett didn't laugh because suddenly it didn't seem funny. "If he did, why would he wait until after the wedding? He could have left her at the altar. Although I'm not sure which is worse."

"Both would be so embarrassing." Violet sat against the dinghy, looking out at the blue expanse. Tilting her head back, she closed her eyes.

"Don't get comfortable. We should get back and let Lexie know we couldn't find her husband."

Sighing, Violet pushed off. The boat tipped, then rocked back into position.

Scarlett gasped.

"What's the matter?" Violet hurried to her side. "You look like you've seen a ghost."

Not wanting to believe her eyes, Scarlett gulped, blood rushed to her head. "Help me turn the boat over."

"Why on earth would we do that?"

With her hands already on the bottom of the dinghy, Scarlett frowned over her shoulder. "Because there's someone under it."

Her sister's eyes widened. "You mean someone's hiding there?"

Scarlett didn't want to destroy the hope for either of them, but it couldn't be avoided. "I don't think anybody's hiding."

Violet paled.

Together they managed to roll the boat over. It thumped down hard, spraying them with sand.

"Chad!" They squealed simultaneously.

The groom stared at the sky and didn't move a muscle. Having seen this before, Scarlett knelt beside him to search for a pulse. "He's dead. Will you run back and get Sam?"

"Gladly." Violet shivered. "It never gets easier to see a dead body, does it?"

Scarlett shook her head. For reasons she refused to think about, they never saw their father after his death five years ago in a logging accident, but their mom died of breast cancer. That was far more horrible to witness, but dead was dead. Chad was a young man with his whole life ahead of him. Newly married, it seemed such a waste. Then there was the why or how. Maybe both.

"Don't say anything to anyone else," she warned. "I'll call the sheriff."

Violet had taken a couple of steps but turned immediately.

"Not to Mr. or Mrs. Turner? Or even, Lexie? What about the Wood family?"

"They all need to know, but it will be better coming from Sam or the sheriff." Scarlett crossed her fingers about that.

CHAPTER THREE

Time ticked by incredibly slowly, and Scarlett checked her watch for the millionth time. Only five minutes had passed since Violet reached the ramp and the steps. That wasn't long. Not really. Except, when you had a dead man at your feet, it seemed forever.

Taking great pains to not get anywhere near Chad, she walked around the immediate area as best she could without disturbing anything. Nate, the local sheriff, would hopefully be pleased with her restraint.

It was interesting that the dinghy was on top of him. He had no marks on his face, so it was conceivable that the boat fell and killed him. Yet, shouldn't Chad be face down if it hit him on the back of the head? It could have been propped up somehow and fallen on him, but it seemed odd that he couldn't crawl out from underneath. Besides, boats didn't get left on their side, did they?

A thousand other questions swirled around inside her head, and the next time she looked up, Sam was running down the beach. Jacket removed, in one hand he carried a bag which banged against his thigh. Paramedics always came with the tools of their trade, regardless of a day off.

Skidding to a halt, short of breath, he landed on his knees beside her.

"I so wanted it to be untrue," his voice wavered. Once he'd frantically checked for a pulse and listened to Chad's chest with a stethoscope, Sam squeezed his eyes shut for a second. His eyelashes became wet, and his lips quivered.

Scarlett touched his shoulder. "I'm so sorry. I know he was your close friend."

"My best friend." Wiping his eyes on the sleeve of his shirt, Sam sighed deeply. "We went to college together, and he offered to share his room with me in the second year, so I had a quieter place to study. It was the one thing he fought his parents over, and because he lives nearby, it was the main reason I chose Cozy Hollow to settle down in."

Scarlett had known that they were close and about them going to college together, but they'd never discussed his motives for moving to town. It turned out there was a lot she didn't know. Her throat felt thick with emotion, but she wanted to be strong for Sam. "Did he suffer from ill-health?"

"Not that I'm aware of. I like to keep fit, but Chad was a bit of a freak about it. Brilliant at nearly everything that needed a racquet or a bat, the only thing I could win against him was online games." He attempted a smile and failed.

"I wonder who would want to kill him?"

Sam reared back from her. "Kill him? What the heck makes you think that he was killed?"

Scarlett gulped, wishing she could take back the words, and she couldn't lie. "It occurred to me that he couldn't have placed the dinghy over himself. If he didn't die because of sickness and didn't appear to have had a heart attack, it had to involve another person?"

She only knew what heart attacks looked like after the

previous librarian in Cozy Hollow had met her demise this way, and Sam had been with Scarlett after she found Mable Norris.

Sam flopped onto his backside as if she'd hit him. "I'd already ruled that out. Without checking him over more thoroughly, I can't say what did kill him." He glanced over his shoulder to where the top of the tent was visible. "I'm not convinced, but if it were due to foul play, that would mean it had to be somebody from the wedding." His eyes narrowed.

Scarlett followed his gaze. "Maybe."

He turned back to her. "Pardon?"

She shrugged. "Someone could have been waiting for Chad, or he could have met up with them on the beach. I believe he's been missing for some time."

"But why would they choose today of all days?" Sam asked with disgust.

She dug her shoes in the sand. "Well, I don't like to mention it, but . . ."

"Just tell me," he asked through gritted teeth.

She flinched at his tone. "He looked so miserable throughout the whole ceremony."

Sam's mouth opened and closed. "Did he?"

"Are you saying you didn't notice it?" Scarlett didn't buy that at all—not if they were such close friends. Why would he lie to her?

He loosened his tie and undid the top button of his shirt as if he couldn't get enough air.

"You do know about his change of heart, don't you?"

He touched Chad's cheek. "I thought he simply had cold feet. Which is perfectly natural."

"Is it?" Scarlett put that in a compartment for future reference. Their dates were mainly conducted at her house or the local park in case he was called to an emergency. At least that was his excuse. Maybe this was a warning for her that he didn't want to get serious, despite what he said when they were occasionally alone. She shook her head to rid it of these selfish thoughts. This was about Chad and Lexie.

"That's what I've heard about weddings," Sam backtracked, before giving her a funny look. "Except, over this last week, I found out that there was more to Chad's reluctance than cold feet."

Scarlett kept her *ah-hah* to herself. "What was it."

Sam looked around guiltily. "Chad was seeing someone else," he whispered.

She grimaced, not wanting to think badly of Sam's best friend. "Then why did he go ahead with the wedding?"

"Because his father threatened to cut him off."

She tilted her head. "Financially?"

Sam nodded miserably. "In every way. Being kicked out of the business would have devastated him. I know it's hard for you to appreciate, but as long as I've known him, Chad never had to worry about money, and he took the idea of one day running the corporation very seriously."

The sound of sirens cut through the conversation, and while they waited expectantly, Scarlett wondered who Chad had preferred to Lexie.

Eventually, Violet led the Sheriff, a deputy, the Turners, and Chad's parents down the beach. When she was close enough, Violet gave her an apologetic look.

Scarlett shrugged. Once the sheriff, Nathaniel Adams, arrived, her sister couldn't be expected to hide what had happened from the Turners. And certainly Lexie, along with Chad's parents, had a right to know what had befallen her new husband.

Sam helped Scarlett to her feet, and they backed away from the body. Chad's mom immediately fell on her son, sobbing loudly. Lexie, arms wrapped around herself, was also crying, a hand to her mouth, she rocked backward and forward.

The Sheriff gently pulled the mom away. "I'm sorry, Mrs. Wood. I need you to move back so we can seal off the area."

"Whatever for?" Mr. Wood blustered.

"Because this is now a crime scene," Nate reasoned patiently.

"A crime scene? Was he murdered? Here?" Mr. Turner asked loudly. He looked around them, clearly affronted that someone could do such a thing on his beach.

Appreciating that people reacted differently to terrible news, nevertheless, Scarlett felt a surge of dislike for the man. The body of his new son-in-law lay a few feet away, and it appeared that all he could think about was the inconvenience Chad's demise made to his life.

Nate stiffened, eyeing the man warily. "At this stage, I can't say whether this is a murder investigation or not. However, I concede that it does look suspicious, and therefore the scene needs to be protected at all costs." The Sheriff nodded to his deputy, who placed a pole in the ground and tied it with yellow tape. Then, looking pointedly at the group, who stepped back with varying degrees of acceptance, he continued to place more poles and tape around the dinghy and Chad.

Mr. Turner harrumphed, while Mrs. Turner surveyed the houses in the distance. Scarlett glanced around. Were they genuinely more concerned with their neighbors knowing what was going on here? Could they not comprehend that, if this turned out to be a murder, everyone at the wedding would be a suspect and that the neighbors would know soon enough? And what about the feelings of their new in-laws who looked devasted?

Ignoring the crowd, once they had indeed moved back, Nate made several passes around the area. Scarlett took note of how carefully he walked in his own tracks. Then, the sheriff went down to the water, which was less than a dozen feet away due to the tide coming in rapidly. Next, he went a little way north and then south of where the dinghy was. When he came back, it was to kneel beside the deceased. Slipping gloves on, he felt in Chad's pocket. Pulling out a phone, he shielded it from the group, studied it for a minute.

When he stood, Nate addressed them solemnly. "Would you all please go back up to the wedding tent. My deputy will come with you to begin asking everyone some questions. It will be one at a time and, Mr. Turner, you need to ensure that no one leaves before they've been spoken to."

"Is that absolutely necessary?" Mr. Turner was outraged. "We'd prefer to deal with this without a couple of hundred people hanging about."

Mr. Wood, an arm around his distraught wife, glared. "My son, your son-in-law, is dead! How do you propose the sheriff finds the murderer without asking questions?"

"There's no need for raised voices," Mrs. Turner snapped. "The sheriff has said he doesn't know what caused this. Let's go back and discuss the situation in a civilized manner."

Mr. Wood wasn't interested in her platitudes. "There will be no discussion, civilized or otherwise, Davina. Our son is dead. On your beach. I want to know the reason why."

Scarlett felt sorry for the couple. If this felt surreal to her, how would it feel to them Knowing their son had died while they were partying? "Of course you do, Sir. Let's let the sheriff do his job to find out. Might I suggest we get back to the house, and I'll make coffee for everyone?"

"Coffee? I need something a darn site stronger than that!" Mr. Turner marched up the beach. "Davina! Lexie!"

His wife hurried after him, dragging poor Lexie, who was still crying. Behind them, at a much slower pace, the Woods followed.

Scarlett and Violet were also about to leave when Nate called out. He'd moved out of the taped area and was writing in a notebook.

"Can you stay, Scarlett? I'd like to hear exactly how you came upon the deceased."

"Of course. Do you need Violet too?"

"I'll talk to her soon, up at the house. It's best if you each tell your own story. Don't discuss this with anyone," he warned Violet.

Her sister nodded, looking relieved to get away.

"Can you organize the coffee or tea?" Scarlett asked. "I'll be there to help as soon as I can."

Violet nodded again and ran back up the beach.

Nerves frayed, Scarlett would have liked to follow, but Nate was waiting. "I'm sorry, I don't think I have much to say that could help."

"Don't apologize. We have to start somewhere, and you did find the body."

She nodded and explained how that had come about as succinctly as she could manage. She'd met Chad a couple of times briefly and only knew what Sam had told her about him. Around her age, the ink barely dry on the wedding certificate, this was tragic, but her heart was also heavy at the sight of Sam's sadness. Struggling to control his emotions, he seemed determined to do his job as a paramedic.

Sam pinched the bridge of his nose. "He's my best friend. More like brothers, really. I can't imagine not having him around."

Nate rubbed his face as if what he was doing just got a great deal more difficult. "I'm sorry, Sam, but I have to ask, you knew him better than most people here?"

Sam nodded. "I liked to think so. Apart from his family."

Scarlett raised an eyebrow, which Nate saw.

"Do you have something you want to tell me, Sam?"

Sam sighed heavily before explaining about Chad's change of heart and Mr. Wood's insistence that the wedding wouldn't be canceled under any circumstances.

Nate wrote quickly but made little in the way of comment, bar a few encouraging noises. When Sam finished talking, Nate studied him for a moment.

"What did you think about your friend marrying someone he didn't love?"

"I don't condone it, but as I said to Scarlett, I honestly thought it was merely cold-feet. I initially believed Chad loved Lexie, and this was just a blip that he'd get over. I only found out recently that there was another woman involved."

"Cold feet doesn't usually kill a person," Nate noted seriously. "Who was this other woman?"

Sam hesitated.

"It can't hurt Chad now," Scarlett reminded him.

"It might hurt Lexie." Sam's anguish made him turn away. "She doesn't deserve anymore hurt right now, but I guess you'd find out from someone else. It's Rebecca Johnson."

"One of the bridesmaids?" Scarlett gasped. Had Lexie known? Surely no one was that good an actress.

Sam nodded.

"Do you think the bride knew?" Nate asked.

Sam took a second or two to think on that, still pale and somewhat shaky "No. I'm pretty sure she was oblivious to it."

"That's what I don't understand," Scarlett mused while thinking that Sam wasn't as convinced as he was trying to sound.

Nate's eyes narrowed. "You have an opinion on that? I believe you didn't know the family well."

His words irritated her. Because they were Sam's friends, she would like to have known Chad and Lexie better. It bothered her more than she'd realized that she didn't. Sam had explained that she wasn't invited as his date because he was to partner with a bridesmaid. Therefore she'd be stuck at another table with strangers and be bored. Then she'd been offered the job and promptly forgot about that aspect. "Yes, I do have my own opinion—despite barely knowing them. Chad wasn't happy at all," she said tersely.

"Love is said to be blind," Nate muttered, pen poised over his paper. "So, how did you get the job?"

Scarlett couldn't understand why Nate was acting so odd about her involvement. It was merely a coincidence that she was here. "Through Sam. The Turner's were desperate, and it was very last minute. The tension over this wedding has been pretty high."

Nate made more notes. "Okay. Carry on."

"Based on my observations over today and the few times we met with Lexie and her mother, I'd say that there are deeper issues than an unhappy groom."

He sighed. "Alright, let's hear it."

"I agree that on the surface, Lexie appears the grieving widow, but she would have had to be blind not to notice Chad's reluctance and even dread about saying I do."

Nate frowned. "That seems in contradiction to the distraught bride I just witnessed."

Scarlett could only nod. "I agree, but you should have seen Chad. Maybe when you've asked your questions, you'll appreciate just how many people would have noticed his demeanor. I assure you—he barely attempted to hide it. Plus, someone might have an insight as to why Lexie didn't want to acknowledge it."

"Maybe that's why this happened?" Sam finally contributed. "If Rebecca and Chad were in love and he went ahead and married Lexie, then someone must have been all kinds of mad."

Nate shook his head. "Unless she's deceptively strong as

an ox, the bridesmaid I saw couldn't overpower this man. Look at him. Chad's huge, and there's nothing of her."

Sam recoiled. "I didn't say it was Rebecca who killed Chad."

"Which would mean there's another motive," Scarlett added.

"If you don't mind, I'm not ruling out anyone." Nate grunted as he pushed the dinghy back over the body.

"Are you looking for clues like footprints?" Scarlett enquired, curious over what he was doing and why.

Nate peered over the top of the boat and raised an eyebrow. "I think both of you should get back to the group. Sam, you might be needed by Mrs. Wood or the bride, and I think it best to leave Chad to the ambulance officers since you're so close to the deceased."

It wasn't a question. With a lingering look at the spot where his friend was, Sam picked up his bag and walked silently with her up the beach. When they reached the steps, something caught Scarlett's eye. As she stopped to retrieve it, a woman appeared at the top.

"Finally. I need you to calm Lexie down, Sam. Now!" Mrs. Turner demanded.

"Good luck," Scarlett whispered.

"I have no idea what I'm supposed to do or say," Sam admitted huskily.

"You've had to deal with bereaved parties before, so I know you'll figure it out." She thought she was encouraging, but Sam glared at her.

He climbed the stairs without replying, leaving Scarlett to wonder why he was determined to take offense to everything she said.

Was she insensitive?

CHAPTER FOUR

U sing a tissue to wrap her find, which turned out to be a man's ring, Scarlett absently tucked it into her apron pocket.

Sam was feeling this deeply, and she wanted to find a way to console him. As soon as she'd dealt with the refreshments and given the ring to Nate, she'd find him and see if she could do just that.

When she reached the top of the stairs, Ruby waited for her. Red-eyed, her youngest sister threw herself into Scarlett's arms. The hug was firm and very mutual.

"It must have been horrific finding Chad like that. Sam was so upset. I thought he was going to break Violet's arm when she told him," Ruby blurted."

Scarlett could only nod. Sam won a scholarship to a college in Destiny that he'd no hope of otherwise attending. Rooming with Chad cemented an immediate friendship, but Sam had never mentioned the actual depth of his feelings before today. It was no wonder he'd kept Chad's secret about another woman, and it wasn't Scarlett's place to judge him or his motives. Not when she'd seen how torn he was that Lexie might suffer because of his silence.

Sam was visible through the crowd of people. He crouched in front of Mrs. Wood and Lexie, who were using tissues by the handful. Mr. Wood and Mr. Turner glared at each other from behind the heads of the women, as if in a western shootout. Meanwhile, Mrs. Turner circulated among the guests.

Now wasn't the time to go to him. Instead, Scarlett hurried to the kitchen with Ruby. Violet must have been watching for them because she bolted out the door with Olivia in tow.

"What should we do?" Violet asked. "The chef has no clue either."

"Nate doesn't want anyone to leave, and the guests will likely be in shock. I suggest we keep supplying coffee and tea. I'll also ask Mrs. Turner if we could offer something stronger."

"Do you need to ask?" Violet gave her a pointed look. "It's not like they don't have plenty at the bar."

"Still, that's not our call." Scarlett saw uncertainty in many of the guests, and some did look like they were making moves to leave. "We can only do our part in ensuring these people stay and don't panic."

"What about the beautiful cake?" Olivia said sorrowfully.

"Good point. I'll ask about that too. They may get hungry again, and it would be a waste not to use it."

"After all that food?" Olivia sounded skeptical.

"It was a feast," Scarlett acknowledged. "But that was a couple of hours ago, and bored people often want to eat. They might have to stay here a while, and those that haven't had the horrific events take their appetite will need something to occupy them while they wait for their turn at being questioned." She shrugged. "Coffee, or something stronger, and cake, will fill in time and might soothe them a little."

Ruby's mouth trembled. "It's so sad that the bride and groom haven't even cut it."

"I don't think we want to mention that to anyone," Scarlett warned.

Violet was less inclined to subtlety. "I'm sure they'll be thinking that when we hand it around."

Scarlett gave Violet a withering look. Sometimes this sister went that little bit too far. "Could you please see to the drinks and do your best not to upset anyone?"

Violet looked ready to argue, but Olivia stepped between them. "You can rely on us, dear. You go ahead and speak to Mrs. Turner about the cake."

"I'm just so glad that I don't have to do it," Ruby agreed gratefully.

Violet had the good grace to look ashamed, and Scarlett left them to it. As the eldest, she always took on these kinds of tasks, because it seemed the right thing to do, which didn't make it any easier. Straightening her back, she smoothed her apron and walked cautiously over to the bride's mother, who sat talking in a low voice with her husband, the bride, and the Woods.

"Excuse me."

The woman sighed at the interruption, which was an improvement on yelling. "What do you need?"

Scarlett bent a little, keeping her voice low. "I'd like to offer our condolences, and along with your staff, we'd like to assist in keeping the guests calm. I wondered if we could hand out brandy and pieces of the wedding cake?" she whispered the last part.

"You want to cut the cake?" Mrs. Turner snarled.

Scarlett winced as several heads turned their way, and

Mrs. Wood wailed into a handful of tissues. Lexie paled to the color of her dress.

Taking a step back, Scarlett kept her face neutral. "It was merely a suggestion to keep the guests occupied while the sheriff does his job."

Lexie stood, wiping her tear-stained cheeks and puffy eyes. "Yes, that's a good idea. Nothing will bring Chad back, and there's certainly no point in keeping the cake. I don't want to look at it again." Head high, she walked through the tent and into the house.

"You have your answer," Mrs. Turner hissed.

Scarlett couldn't wait to get away and hightailed it back to the kitchen. As much as she was sorry for the family, the woman was like Medusa, and no one should have to experience her bite more than necessary.

Passing through clusters of guests, who were discussing the wedding and the death, wasn't a pleasant experience either. Some sounded almost gleeful that this had happened. One man in particular, who wore a tailored black suit, and wore a large gold ring, suggested that the Turner's being taken down a peg or two was overdue. She tried to get a closer look at that ring, which looked an awful lot like the one in her pocket, but he inconveniently put his hands behind his back. The group of men, similarly attired around him, shifted awkwardly but didn't challenge the inappropriate comment.

As she continued, Scarlett tried to imprint his face on her brain. Several, from other groups, complained at being detained unreasonably, and she couldn't stop a few tuts escaping.

Wow! Surely some of them liked the Turners and Woods? If not, then why would they attend this ceremony? What seemed on the surface like a perfect wedding, not so long ago, now appeared tacky and tainted by the undercurrent.

Not that death wouldn't affect them, but sorrow wasn't the only emotion present. Or even the most prevalent. At this rate of unrest, the poor sheriff would have a tough job making sure no one left.

As if she'd summoned him, Nate appeared briefly with Mr. Turner before they disappeared down the hall. Assuming the father of the bride was one of the first on the list to be questioned, this was going to be a long evening.

Although she couldn't be sure, the numbers looked less than earlier. The deputy had dealt with a few guests in the room by the front door. However, this was not the only exit.

She couldn't see Nate right this minute, but she'd seek him out as soon as he came out again. The ring could be a vital piece of evidence.

Scarlett pulled her focus back to the cake. The chef had everything under control with the aftermath of feeding so many people. Finishing cleaning down his kitchen with the help of his staff, the wait staff hung around the door, unsure of their role.

Those guests who were insensitive to Chad's death could make things ugly. *Uglier,* she corrected her thoughts. They should be occupied and so should the staff.

"Chef, would you mind cutting the cake and keeping the tea and coffee going? My team will take it out if the wait staff could handle drinks. Brandy would be best, but whatever they prefer is fine."

He gave her a withering glance. "Are you in charge now, Missy? Because my staff are getting ready to leave."

The kitchen team had most been amicable until now, and while Scarlett understood that he was king of his kitchen, she also had a job to do. She guessed that he was probably not used to taking suggestions from anyone but his employer. Therefore, why would he want to listen to someone at half his age?

"I assure you that's not the case." Scarlett opted for a tactic that was a little underhanded. "I'm simply following Mrs. Turner's directions. Did you want to speak to her yourself? I could get her?"

Instantly his haughtiness evaporated. "No. That's fine. Naturally, we'll be happy to work as long as Mrs. Turner needs us."

"I know she'll be grateful." Scarlett smiled pleasantly.

He raised a bushy eyebrow, then sent two of his staff to bring the cake back to the kitchen. It was a wise move— cutting it in front of everyone would be in poor taste.

Violet, Ruby, and Olivia had observed the proceedings, and with a flick of her head, Scarlett beckoned them into the corner by the pantry. Huddling together, Scarlett explained that along with the staff, the four of them would interact with the guests to ensure they were comfortable by handing out more drinks and the cake.

Not even Violet disagreed. "I can't wait to get out of here."

"I know," Scarlett agreed. "But we won't be able to leave until Nate decides, so we may as well keep busy."

"I don't mind helping. It's so awful this happened on what was supposed to be such a happy day." Ruby gulped, and Olivia put an arm around her shoulders.

"I just wish we knew what happened to Chad and why."

"I know that look. You're going to try to find out, aren't you?" Violet retorted.

Scarlett glanced around the room. The chef and his staff were cutting the cake and laying it onto individual plates on the other side of the room.

"For goodness sake, talk quieter," she hissed. "I admit that I have a bad feeling that some of the guests might cause problems, and I think we could circumvent it or hear some-thing that could help the case if we're among them."

"And if we did, we would tell the sheriff as soon as possible." Olivia sounded pleased to be involved in a little intrigue.

"Definitely. We don't personally act on anything we hear," Scarlett emphasized.

Ruby nodded. "I guess that would be okay."

"As long as you don't expect us to interrogate anyone?"

Violet's narrowed gaze made Scarlett uncomfortable.

"I'm merely saying that it's an opportunity to glean information, and we should be prepared to take mental notes if it does happen."

"Hmmm."

Due to the family's involvement in a couple of crimes recently, Violet was justifiably distrustful of Scarlett's intentions. It probably wasn't prudent right now to point out that her sisters had been just as keen on solving those cases as she was. "Let's get started on handing out the cake."

With her family all roughly on the same page, they soon had a production team going. Along with the staff, they loaded trays of cake with cups, saucers, tea, and coffee.

Scarlett delegated Ruby and Violet areas for serving, making sure to take the ones where the Woods and Turners were for herself.

Away from the leading group, Mr. Wood, a big man like his son, had folded in on himself. He looked up as she approached, then nodded when she held up the tray questioningly.

"Sybil, have a cup of tea, dear."

His wife, the only other person at the small table, turned away. "I don't want anything. Why did this happen to my beautiful boy? I told you he shouldn't have to marry her!" Mrs. Wood wailed anew. "He even took her name."

Scarlett was shocked. Taking the Turner name was a big move from these very by-the-book families. Mrs. Wood did not appear to be a fan of that decision.

Her husband grimaced at the horrible sound. "Shush. A bit of dignity, please."

Mrs. Wood stiffened at his hand on her shoulder. "Don't touch me, Paul. And don't you talk to me about dignity. Chad's death is all your fault. I will never forgive you."

Perplexed and a little intrigued, Scarlett awkwardly placed half the contents of the tray on the table. "Maybe later," she said gently.

The couple ignored her, and each other, so she continued to the next seating, her mind whirring. Forced marriage, infidelity, and a change in surname. Which of these was to blame for the troubles today? Or was it compounded issues? When he had a moment, she'd give this information to Nate —as well as the ring, which felt heavy in her pocket.

Glancing around the tent, mainly to check on her family, Scarlett neared Mrs. Turner, who was speaking to two other women who had gathered around her in a tight circle. Suddenly, something registered that made Scarlett pause. She hadn't seen the groomsmen, or the bridesmaids since she got back from the beach.

Just then, Mr. Turner stormed out of the house. Marching across the tent, he pushed passed Scarlett, almost upsetting the pots of hot liquid. She steadied the clatter and looked up to find the group eyeing her distastefully.

Having gained the attention of his wife, Mr. Turner, pointed back the way he'd come. It looked like Nate was ready for his next interview.

Davina Turner retraced her husband's steps with the air of someone who has an unpleasant job to do but will soldier on regardless, without acknowledging anyone else.

Scarlett handed her half-empty tray to a staff member with instructions of who to serve. Then, acting on a hunch, she went through the kitchen and slipped down the hall.

CHAPTER FIVE

The house was just as impressive as the first time she'd seen it at her interview for catering the wedding and subsequent meetings. Unfortunately, devoid of Chad or Lexie's light and laughter, the place lost its attractiveness. Now, the richness seemed gaudy and useless—and cold.

The way the Turners behaved and treated people, just went to prove that a beautiful house didn't necessarily make a person happy. Even the appeal of so many intricate and exquisite carvings she'd earlier noticed on every side-table and available space faded.

In the opposite direction to the kitchen at the furthest end of the hall was a large conservatory. As she got closer, Scarlett saw a flash of white through the glass doors. Again, she felt the lump of tissue in her pocket. This was just what she was looking for. Or, to be more precise, whom.

Late afternoon sunlight shone through the glass roof, making her fair hair sparkle as Lexie paced the conservatory. Even in her sadness, she was beautiful. The few times they'd met, Scarlett had also thought her very sweet. How could Chad not love her?

Lexie rubbed her hands together, over and over, muttering something, but Scarlett couldn't make out what she was saying.

"Lexie?" she called softly so as not to startle her.

Turning quickly, Lexie cried out as if she couldn't contain herself. "This is all my fault."

Scarlett hadn't imagined that Lexie would talk to her so easily, but she certainly wasn't about to pass up the chance to hear what she had to say. "How can this possibly be your fault?"

Lexie took a deep breath. "If only I'd listened to Chad, it wouldn't have happened."

"You don't know that, and you didn't kill him." Scarlett wasn't sure this was true, but it seemed incredibly unlikely.

"I could never do that." Lexie's voice was full of anguish. "I loved him. I thought everyone else did too."

"People do bad things in the name of love," Scarlett suggested.

"So many people," Lexie agreed with a heavy sigh. Her face suddenly darkened. "You have no idea what it's like always to have to do the right thing. I knew marrying Chad was wrong, but there was nothing either of us could do."

Scarlett's skin tingled. The situation had been awful for both of them. And to what purpose had their parents decided on a future that would make their children miserable? Surely, the opposite was how it was supposed to be?

"Do you have someone to talk to about this? A close friend, or your mom?"

Lexie laughed bitterly. "My mom isn't the kind of person you discuss feelings with, and my parents insisted my "friends" are always the children of their peers. I wouldn't tell any of them my secrets if my life depended on it."

Scarlett was deeply moved that Lexie was trusting her, an almost stranger, with those very secrets. This beautiful woman was the definition of a poor little rich girl. Or, a bird in a gilded cage.

"I'm sorry, Lexie. If you want to talk, I'd be glad to listen anytime."

The room was quiet as Lexie studied her for a moment. "Why would you? You don't even know me."

"I know what Sam's told me, and I trust him. Also, what's happened to you is awful, and I happen to have some experience in awful."

Lexie made a sympathetic noise. "Sam said you lost both your parents. Your mom not so long ago?"

Intrigued that Sam had discussed her with his friends, Scarlett nodded.

"My father was killed in a logging accident five years ago, and my mom passed away from cancer. It's been nearly a year." The words were a physical pain. Those moments in time were hard to remember without breaking into tiny pieces. While she was getting better at dealing with them day to day, talking about her parents made it feel like it happened yesterday.

Lexie put a hand on her arm. "I'm sorry. Were you close?"

"Very." Scarlett chewed her bottom lip.

"But, you still have your sisters?"

Scarlett had to smile, despite the ache inside her. "Yes. They keep me on an even keel most of the time."

"That must be nice. I mean, to have sisters would be great," Lexi said wistfully. "Someone to share things with."

"We have our days when it's not so good—but not too often. Quite frankly, I couldn't manage the café without them." Scarlett didn't mention that she hated the thought they might one day leave Cozy Hollow.

Lexi tilted her head. "What's that like—the café ?"

"Hard work. Fun. Hard work," Scarlett half-joked,

wondering how the conversation had so easily slipped away from Lexie.

Lexie managed a half-smile. "But you wouldn't do anything else?"

"I truly can't imagine anything other than what I do. I love everything about it. My sisters aren't so passionate," Scarlett admitted.

"No?"

Scarlett shrugged. "They have other dreams."

"Does that upset you?"

"It did." It seemed that Scarlett was having a session with a therapist. It was odd, but she couldn't upset Lexie when she so obviously needed to talk about something other than Chad's death. She'd let it run for a few more moments before getting back to the topic Scarlett would rather discuss. "Until I realized that we each have to make our own way in the world, and my way is not the only one." There'd been a light-bulb moment that made her see this truth and made it easier for them to move on.

Lexie squeezed Scarlett's arm rather hard. "Exactly! I'd love to be able to do that. To find my happy place and be good at something and not just decoration."

Scarlett struggled to hide her surprise at the heartfelt anguish. Surely with unlimited funds at her disposal, Lexie could have trained to be anything. Believing she already knew the answer, she asked anyway, "Do you have a job?"

"Me?" Lexie scoffed. "My job was to catch a wealthy husband. Look how that turned out," her voice shook again. "Like I said, I knew it was wrong to marry Chad. We actually liked each other as people, and we were good together, you know?"

Puzzled, Scarlett could only nod.

"We also liked many of the same things, and we hardly argued." Lexie pulled an orchid from a magnificent plant and twirled it in agitated fingers. "Growing up together in the same circles, doing the same things, the way our parents insisted, we were model children and teenagers. Marriage was the last step to join our perfect lives."

The words poured from the bride until she vibrated with deep anger, and Scarlett thought she understood. "Do you mean it was an arranged marriage?"

"Of course." Lexie nodded. "Chad was my friend first. All I wanted from him was to keep our relationship that way. I'd rather have married someone like Sam."

Scarlett developed a sudden coughing fit. "Sam?" she croaked.

Lexie almost smiled. "Don't worry. I know you two are a thing. I just meant I'd prefer someone who didn't follow conventions. Someone with a bit more—spark. Someone who would make me feel for him the way a man and a woman are supposed to."

Spark? Sam? What did that even mean? Sam was as down to earth as any man Scarlett had met. There was nothing spark like about him. Except for the way he made her feel when they were together. Safe. Warm.

"I can't believe I'm talking like this when poor Chad is lying out there on the sand. Dead." Tears cascaded down Lexie's cheeks once more. "There's something wrong with me."

Scarlett tutted. "Don't be so hard on yourself. You're in shock, and that makes a person say things they might not at any other time."

"Who else can I be hard on?" Lexie asked as if she were grabbing a lifeline.

"The person who killed him," Scarlett suggested. "If that's what happened."

"Chad was as healthy as a horse." Lexie stopped crying and glared over her tissue. "So, it had to be murder, didn't it?

But who would do that? I don't know anyone capable of such a thing."

"You know all of the people out there." Scarlett pointed in the rough direction of the back garden. "It would be fair to assume if it was murder, that it could be one of the guests."

"You'd think I would know all the people at my wedding, but I don't. Very few of them are family members. Most are our parents' friends and business partners," Lexie's voice wobbled again. "Although many of them think we're one big family."

Scarlett tapped her nails together. It wasn't going to be easy to bring up the things that bugged her, but she forged ahead as gently as possible. "There's a large man out there with a black suit."

Lexie blinked a couple of times, and Scarlett almost slapped her own forehead. What was she thinking? It was a wedding; therefore, plenty of men wore dark suits today.

"Sorry. The man I'm thinking of has a fancy gold ring. It has crossed axes on the top, and it's pretty big. Does that mean anything to you?"

"There will be several men wearing that ring today. Probably all wearing dark suits," Lexie said thoughtfully. "They belong to the club."

Naturally, Scarlett was intrigued but kept her face neutral. "What kind is it? An elite club?"

Lexie initially looked blank as if she didn't understand the concept, then she shrugged. "I guess it is because not everyone is allowed to join. My father and Chad's father belong to it."

"What about Chad?"

"He will belong once he begins working for my father." Lexie's eyes welled up. "I mean, he would have been allowed in by then."

Things were getting weirder. Pretty sure that the ring in

her pocket was identical to the one worn by the man now, it turns out there were more out there. However, if the ring wasn't Chad's, then someone else was missing theirs?

"So everyone who works for your dad gets a ring?"

Lexie hiccupped. "Only select people are invited into the club."

Confident that this was somehow important to the case, Scarlett deliberately kept her voice light. "How do you get selected?"

Lexie blinked her baby blues again. "Mom always said it's just men being boys, and I shouldn't worry about their silliness. I know that every member must attend the same schools and belong to one of the Carver families. Why?"

With the openness of this conversation, Scarlett gained an insight into Lexie's upbringing, but this level of compliance made her shudder. They weren't close friends, and Mrs. Turner would probably not approve if they were, but it seemed that Lexie had been forced into a persona that wasn't a perfect fit.

Lexie sounded as if she was sorry she'd not questioned her mom further. Had she suddenly decided to rebel, and getting rid of Chad was the only way left to her?

Scarlett sucked in air, not as composed as she'd like to be, yet unable to stop. "I've been wondering about, Sam. He doesn't have a ring, does he?"

Lexie looked down. "Chad did ask on his behalf, but Sam isn't, you know—a businessman or part of the Carver community."

If it hadn't been clear before then, it was abundantly so now. Select could mean in the right class, but it certainly implied in the right business and having the right blood. And, by the way she said it, despite giving the impression that she was a good daughter and listened to her parents, Lexie didn't approve.

Maybe they didn't know each other well, but Scarlett would place a bet that Lexie was a decent person. Not unkind, or mean like her mom, she spoke pleasantly to the staff without condescension and had treated Scarlett and her sisters well. Any thoughts that she could have harmed Chad simply didn't feel right.

Scarlett nodded sympathetically. "If that's the criteria, it makes some sense. Although his job is important. Anyway, this isn't the time to talk about such things, and I've taken enough of your time. Will you be okay by yourself, or should I get someone to come and stay with you?"

Eyes wide, Lexie backed away. "Thank you so much for staying a while, and trying to take my mind off things, but I'd rather be alone now."

Scarlett watched her walk to the far end of the conservatory, where it looked over a small man-made lake. There was no sparkle left in her eyes, and she'd watched Lexie fold into herself with each step. No one could fake this level of pain. A pain that Scarlett remembered too well when she and her sisters had lost both their parents.

It was time to find Nate. And interrupt him if necessary.

CHAPTER SIX

The hall was empty as she slowly retraced her steps, checking rooms along the way. There was a library on the right with a study directly opposite. Both were empty. Checking both ways, Scarlett slipped inside the library. It was massive. Dark, broody hand-carved figurines of varying sizes, lined several shelves. Four large pictures graced the far wall where a sizeable hand-carved desk sat in front, dominating the room. Even the chair behind it was fit for a president or a king with its burgundy richness. The leather was smooth and shiny on the armrests and also where a head must have leaned many times.

Scarlett went closer to see the pictures more clearly. There was a sense of familiarity about two of them, although all four men depicted in each frame looked very stern. Dressed in the same dark suits, they looked down on her in a way that reminded her she shouldn't be there.

Taken at different times, the suits' style in each frame reminded her of specific decades, as did the haircuts and facial hair. There was a common theme of dark suits, but also the men in each one appeared to be roughly the same age as each other.

Voices reached her from the hall, interrupting her fascination. Creeping to the door, she inched her head around the opening to find Mr. Wood and Nate facing each other. The groom's father had his hands clenched at his sides, and even from several feet away, Scarlett noticed he was red-faced. It was unclear if it was merely from his anger or that fact that he'd knocked back a little more brandy than he should.

"May I remind you that our son is dead. I wish to take my wife home, not wait about while you do your job. You've spoken to both of us, and she needs to rest. We also have arrangements to make." His voice was cold, and there was a noticeable slurring.

"I was just about to say," Nate said coolly, "that you may both leave. Please stay by a phone and don't leave town in case we need to talk further. And you should have someone drive you," he added firmly.

Mr. Wood sniffed. "I don't know what you're implying, but I have a driver."

He stormed off. At least that looked like his intention. Instead, he managed to sway into one wall, bounce off, and hit the other. Twice.

"Pssst."

Nate turned quickly and frowned at the sight of Scarlett in the library doorway. She put a finger to her lips and beckoned him with her other hand.

He was beside her in several strides, pushing her back into the room and knocking the door, almost closing it with his heel. "What are you doing back here?"

Scarlett flushed a little at his manhandling and the stern tone. "I've been talking to the bride."

He towered over her. "Why would you do that?"

She took a step back. The room was decidedly cooler.

"You were busy, and I had a hunch that I thought important enough to act on. The moment presented itself when I saw Lexie all alone in the conservatory," she reasoned.

"It's my job to have the hunches," he growled.

She crossed her arms. "Surely that doesn't preclude anyone else from getting them, Sheriff?"

His sigh was deep and long. "What do you know, Scarlett?"

She ignored his ruffled feathers. "Well, first of all, the marriage was arranged."

"I've already ascertained that."

"Really? I can't picture anyone here admitting it," she wondered aloud.

He shrugged. "Let's just say it didn't need spelling out."

She nodded while betting the bride's parents had been very evasive on the subject. Somebody he'd spoken to, or one of his deputies? That would narrow it down since Nate had undoubtedly made it his job to talk to the four families himself. The exasperation on his face made it clear that he wasn't interested in sharing information with her.

"Is that it?" he asked.

"Ah, no. Fishing in her pocket, Scarlett pulled out the tissue and dropped it into Nate's hand. "Lexie also explained to me about these rings. They . . ."

Nate unwrapped it carefully but didn't let her finish. "I've seen this before, and I know that most of the families wear them."

His attitude was wearing a little thin, and knowing he wasn't going to be happy, she blurted how she came to have it. "When you said I could leave the beach, I found this one at the bottom of the steps."

"When and why didn't you tell me before now?"

His annoyance made her flustered. "Firstly, I was waiting for you to come back from the beach, and the deputies were already beginning their questioning. Secondly, I intended to get you alone to hand it over, but you were so busy, and that's when I found Lexie. There was absolutely no intention to hold onto the ring this long."

He let her protestation slide. "So, this is Chad's ring?"

She shook her head. "That's the conclusion I jumped to, but it wasn't."

Nate ran his fingers through his hair. "How can you be sure?"

Scarlett explained about Chad's inclusion in the group being a mere formality, but not actioned yet.

"Wow. I thought that stuff about sororities or groups like this were made up or exaggerated for the movies. I guess in some respects my life's been a little sheltered," he said sheepishly

Surprised at his admission, and wondering for the first time about Nate's background, Scarlett could only agree. "I know what you mean. I felt like I was straight out of Hicksville when Lexie told me. Then I recalled that Ruby got invited into a sorority when she went to college."

His eyebrows shot up almost to his hairline. "I heard she went to college in Destiny, although I can't picture Ruby involved in all that hype."

"You're right. She received a scholarship and determined to get her degree with honors, so Ruby turned it down. Quite frankly, after hearing all about it first-hand, I'm pretty glad she did."

"If she were my sister, I would be too." The animosity finally melted, and Nate managed a smile. "Thanks for the information and the ring. My deputies are doing a good job, and we've let some guests leave already, but there's still too many to question, so I need to give them a hand." He gave her a wry grin. "It's a shame you don't have a license. I could do with another pair of hands. You seem to know automatically who to talk to and what questions to ask."

She knew he was teasing but, if she were honest, Scarlett was flattered. People did tend to talk to her and working in her café she'd heard all sorts of secrets that she kept locked away.

"There is one other thing. Did you know that Chad changed his name to Turner?"

"Another omission. To what purpose? Is there one honest person here?" he muttered as they walked through the kitchen and into the tent.

It seemed that she wasn't the only one thinking the waters were being deliberately muddled, and the first thing she noticed when they entered was that the Turners weren't here. She must have been gone a lot longer than she'd thought because the groups of guests had thinned.

Situated in several corners, what appeared to be a full contingency of Deputies were taking notes and talking quietly to guests seated beside them. A sound she knew drew her attention to the ramp down to the beach where Sam and another man dressed in white appeared. Wheeling a gurney, they kept their eyes firmly ahead and moved at a fast pace up the path and around the side of the house.

Sam still looked shaken, which caused her heart to wrench. She wasn't an expert by any stretch of the imagination, but surely it had taken a long time to get Chad ready for the coroner's van. Perhaps Sam had taken time to compose himself or to say his goodbyes.

As a paramedic, he was used to dealing with many things, but Chad's death was far more personal and, therefore, different from any other case. It was awful that Sam had to deal with it at all in a professional capacity, instead of only as a grieving friend.

Hopefully, it wouldn't be too long before she could have a

moment with him to offer her support. He would surely seek her out when he was ready, and if not, she would find him. And this time she'd do better.

Right now, she needed her sisters. They were better at dealing with tragedy together than apart.

CHAPTER SEVEN

I t was dark by the time Scarlett dropped Olivia at the rear of Cozy Crafts. Like the Cozy Café, many of the local businesses had adopted Cozy in their names, which although a little quirky, tourists loved it.

Ruby made sure their aunt was safe before they headed home as per Nate's instructions when he'd noticed how exhausted they all were. Stating he'd come by in the morning, they were relieved that he hadn't wanted them to stay longer or go to the station.

Scarlett was looking forward to being off her feet and also having a little quiet so she could mull over the events of this troubling day.

Instead, they barely got inside the house on Berry Lane, when Violet demanded answers. "You disappeared for ages. What were you doing all that time?"

With a groan, Scarlett kicked off her shoes and sat heavily on the nearest kitchen chair. "Talking to Lexie."

The other two took seats opposite.

"How was she?" Ruby asked. "I didn't see her for the rest of the evening."

"Not good," Scarlett said sadly. "We were right about the two of them having problems."

Violet tapped the table. "But that's not the end of it. What else do you know?"

"What do you mean?" Not sure what she should divulge, Scarlett played for time.

"Don't be coy, Scarlett. You disappeared for ages, and that can only mean that you have information, and we're not going to bed until you tell us what it is."

Scarlett looked away. "I don't know if I should tell you."

"Why on earth not?" Violet demanded. "We're just as much a part of this as you."

"I'm not trying to hide anything, but I don't want to cloud the case by talking about things that I don't know for sure are true."

Ruby plucked at Scarlett's hand across the table. "If Lexie told you things, they'd have to be true."

Scarlett interlaced their fingers. "Not everyone is as honest as you."

"From what I know about Lexie, she's a lovely person," Ruby insisted. "The few times I met her, she was so nice to me and even offered a donation when I was running low on books after the previous librarian banned some of the children."

"You never told us about that." Scarlett looked to Violet, who shook her head in confirmation that she was also ignorant of this fact.

"Lexie didn't want it known." Ruby frowned. "Sam mentioned it to her and Chad, and they were keen to help, but Lexie intimated that her parents might not approve."

"In helping disadvantaged children?" Violet's eyebrows touched. "That doesn't seem right."

Scarlett tutted. "Having met Lexie's parents, can you

honestly say that they'd like their only child to hang out with poor families?"

"Now that you remind me, I guess they are pretty class orientated," Violet agreed. "Still, children's needs should be above all that."

"I think so too." Scarlett sighed. There would be no sleep until she came clean. "Okay, I'll tell you everything if you promise to keep this between Nate and us."

Ruby clenched her hands on the table. "Nate? This sounds serious."

Scarlett nodded. "It is." While she repeated the conversation with Lexie, her sisters were silent. Then she told them about finding the ring and also what it looked like.

"So you found a ring of Chad's by the stairs, only it turns out to not be Chad's?" Ruby liked to be sure she understood.

"That's right. The rings are only given to members of the corporation when they reach a certain level."

"Like being on the board?" Violet asked.

Scarlett nodded. "I'd say so, although Lexie wasn't sure of the criteria."

Ruby squeezed Scarlett's fingers. "So the murderer was one of the four families?"

Scarlett nodded.

"How awful, but it makes sense." Violet chewed her bottom lip.

"On a positive note, if that's true, it would help to narrow things down. I can't picture Mr. Wood killing his son either, so that's one off the list."

"Apart from the ring, why couldn't it be a woman?" Ruby asked.

Scarlett had sat back, wondering who else they could dismiss, so this didn't help. In fact, it doubled the range of possible murderers. "It could be a woman because we also don't know if the ring is actually a clue or if it was simply dropped. Then again, I'm convinced that one woman couldn't have lifted that boat." Scarlett turned to Violet. "Remember how heavy it was?"

Violet nodded. "Although both the bridesmaids disappeared at the same time."

"That's true," Ruby said. "Where do you suppose they went?"

Scarlett could appreciate how hard this case was going to be for Nate. "I don't know, but I would like to find out. They're around your ages, do either of you know them?"

Ruby frowned. "I went to college with Ellen Wood. We roomed in the same building, but naturally, she didn't have to share a room. We did have a couple of classes and occasionally studied together. She was timid, and I think her brothers, who were both older, gave her a hard time about boys and dating. Her mom was always checking up on her too."

"Maybe they were simply worried about a young girl being away from home?" Scarlett pointed out.

Ruby raised an eyebrow. "All my family checked up on me, but you weren't calling five times a day."

While they digested this, Violet got up to make coffee. She shrugged when Ruby questioned her choice. "It's not like we'll be getting to sleep even if we do get to bed any time soon."

Scarlett approved. "I can't remember having a break all day, and coffee will be very welcome. Anybody know anything about the other bridesmaid?"

"Rebecca and Ellen hung out a lot at college. I got the impression that they were encouraged to since they both lived in Harmony Beach. They were so different, though, and I'm sure that Ellen would have preferred not to be so close."

Scarlett pictured the attractive women in the wedding

party but hadn't noticed any animosity. "What do you mean?"

Uncomfortable speaking negatively about others, Ruby squirmed, but the others waited, and eventually, she explained.

"Rebecca had a very high opinion of herself. When she found out early on that I wasn't rich and had a scholarship, she never bothered with me again, while Ellen didn't seem to care."

"What a snob," Violet retorted. "She was the one who missed out on having you for a friend."

Ruby smiled at her sister's defensiveness and support. "I wasn't bothered in the slightest, but I did feel sorry for Ellen, who seemed very lonely. Anyway, I don't think we can really appreciate how wealthy those families are or the bonds they have, forced or not. The college in Destiny is a good one because the Carver Corporation regularly donates to keep standards high, and all the children from those families go there so they'll be closer to home."

Violet placed steaming cups on the table. "I guess that's good for the rest of the students. Are those families all on the same level of wealth?"

Ruby screwed up her nose. "I'm not sure. The Turners have the bulk of power, but all four families could buy and sell Cozy Hollow many times over. At least, that's what Rebecca said, and Ellen didn't disagree, though she was embarrassed by that conversation."

"Clearly, I've been living in a bubble because I never imagined we had such wealth in this part of Oregon. I guess that's what the club is all about—fostering their corporation and increasing their joint finances," Violet mused. "Working and living so close to each would be kind of weird."

Scarlett snorted. "Is that so?"

Realizing what she'd said, Violet chuckled. "We're different. Besides, there's only three of us, and there must be a couple of dozen over those houses."

Scarlett thought of herself standing on the beach looking up at the amazing houses beyond the dunes. They all had extensive gardens, but in the scheme of things, they were close together. "I suppose having a club could make sense."

Violet peered over the top of her mug. "How does any sort of elitist club make sense?"

"I grant you, I wouldn't like it in Cozy Hollow, but having all that money, perhaps it's a way to show who can be trusted."

Ruby clutched a hand to her chest. "Everyone should be trusted no matter how much money they have until they've indicated otherwise."

Scarlett sat straighter. Playing devil's advocate wasn't moving this forward. "You're absolutely right. Only, not everyone understands that. Including those in the inner circle who decided on a wedding that both the bride and groom objected to."

"But, Lexie looked so happy!" Ruby protested.

Scarlett put a hand up. "She was happy to be getting married and out from under her parents strict rules. The problem was that she'd have preferred someone else as her groom."

"Did she say those exact words?" Violet narrowed her eyes.

Scarlett finished her coffee. "Actually, she said she'd have preferred to marry someone like Sam."

Her sisters gasped as she expected they would. "Relax, she wasn't intentionally hurtful."

"But she knows you and Sam are a thing, and she said it anyway," Violet protested. "That's not right. Nor is mentioning it when Chad is barely cold."

"It was merely a comparison to help explain that Chad,

who was a wonderful man, wasn't right for her." Scarlett groaned. "Stop looking at me like that, Vi. I'm fine about it, so you should be too."

Violet made a rude sound. "If you say so, but it must have been pretty awkward?"

Scarlett hesitated. "A little. Lexie was so distraught, and she probably wouldn't even recall what she said. We all know how that is. Words come out that shouldn't, and everyone gets embarrassed, but eventually, it's all forgotten."

As usual, Ruby jumped in to smooth the water. "Absolutely, and it was a terrible thing to happen, even if she didn't love him."

They were going around in circles, and when Scarlett couldn't think of anything new to add or confess, she yawned, setting off a chain reaction. "Let's get some sleep. My mind is mush right now, and things may be clearer in the morning."

Her sisters agreed and a while later as she lay in her bed. Bob's weight squashed her feet in a warm and comforting manner, and the dog began to snore lightly as she tried to think of something other than Chad's demise.

In particular, how she could help Sam with his tragic loss.

CHAPTER EIGHT

Nate was on their doorstep bright and early. At least the day was bright, and he was certainly early. Heavy-eyed Scarlett dropped the curtain in the sitting room and dragged herself to the door.

Bob greeted Nate with a good deal of sniffing, while George wound around his legs so that he almost fell in the door. Luckily, the sheriff had good balance.

"Come in," Scarlett smiled, hoping he wasn't going to lambast her while preparing herself for precisely that.

Rubbing his dark stubble, he leaned closer. "You look terrible."

"Charming," she uttered without taking offense. The mirror had already shown her that truth, and she didn't feel great either.

"Seriously, are you okay?" He rubbed his hands over Bob's back without taking his eyes off her.

"I'm not sick, but I hardly slept a wink thinking about who the murderer could be. And that you weren't impressed with my input. Apart from that, I'm a box of fluffy ducks."

Nate shook his head, wearily. "You do know that we're not telling the whole of Cozy Hollow that it's murder?"

"Sure," she headed to the kitchen and collected the coffee pot from the stove. "Only, we both know it had to be and the way the people at the wedding closed ranks, I'm convinced everyone there believes that's what it was.."

He grumbled to himself while she poured the brew into two mugs, and they sat across from each other at the table. Nate closed his eyes as he sipped, making her smile again. That first cup was always a pleasure trip for her too. Although this was cup number three for her, it was just as enjoyable.

His eyes shot open. "Darned if I wasn't about to nod off. So, did you remember anything else?"

The slight sarcasm to his tone made her gulp. "Not really. The three of us talked some more when we got home. I know you said not to discuss it, but that's hard when you live in the same house, and I think you'll find what Ruby had to say is very interesting," She babbled.

Nate frowned. "Ruby? How on earth can she be involved in all of this?"

"She went to college with Ellen and Rebecca and had a small, but I think relevant appreciation for their history."

Tucking his gloves into a ball, Nate placed his mug on the table and took out his notebook, flipping several pages. "Are you talking about the bridesmaids?"

Scarlett nodded. "Ruby can tell you herself when she gets out of the shower, but I think the clues all point to the arranged marriage being the catalyst for Chad's demise."

"You do?" he challenged. "And here I thought that this case would be hard to solve."

She blushed. "I didn't mean to imply it was going to be easy, but there's plenty to start with, isn't there?"

He sighed. "Believe me when I say that there's so much to

check, so many people who want to remain close-mouthed, that this case could take months to crack. Things have to be done a certain way, and while we put most of our resources into solving this crime, others are happening in and around Cozy Hollow."

Scarlett put her mug down and twisted her hands on the table. "That's why I'd like to offer my services, as we discussed."

Nate rolled his eyes, then finished his drink. "Hold the phone. We discussed nothing of the sort. I made a throw-away comment, meant as a joke. Anyway, you have a business to run, so how about you leave this to me?"

She merely arched her brow because she'd heard this before, and she didn't want to antagonize him so early in the day. "Will you at least talk to Ruby?"

He nodded wearily. "I'm here to talk to all of you."

"Well, start with me," Violet took a seat next to Scarlett, startling Nate. "Not that I'll have much to add to *Agatha's tale* over here."

Nate's mouth twitched. "Just tell me everything from the beginning—as if you never discussed the case with each other. Scarlett, you can stay, but please don't interrupt. Better yet, don't say anything at all."

Scarlett pretended to zipper her mouth before collecting the coffee pot to top up their cups and pour one for Ruby. Sitting quietly as asked, she listened to Violet's version of the story she now knew by heart.

Just as Violet was winding up, Ruby joined them. With the same directive issued to Violet, Nate questioned Ruby. His notebook was getting a lot of use.

Scarlett was last to give her version of the events, and she tried to relay them as if it were the first time, so she didn't omit anything.

Finally, he tapped the page. "I think I have everything, but call me if you remember any detail, no matter how small."

Scarlett saw him to the door. "I suppose you'll have more people to visit today."

He grimaced. "Most of the bridal party were tight-lipped last night. I'll have to talk to all of them again, but I can't imagine that they'll have any changes of heart about being open about everything."

"That's a shame because it will only delay finding the murderer and surely they do want that. Maybe Sam could make a difference since he knows them all?" she added.

"I spoke to him briefly last night, but he was naturally upset and not terribly communicative."

Scarlett nodded sadly. "He and Chad were so close, it's no wonder he's devastated. I wish I could do something to ease his suffering."

Nate studied her carefully. "You haven't been in touch with Sam since you left the beach?"

"No, the last time I saw him, he was leaving with the body. I've left a ton of messages, and Sam knows he can call me if he wants to talk. I figure he needs some time alone to digest everything. I'll stop by his place later today, but I'd appreciate it if you'd tell him we're all thinking about him and Lexie." Her throat threatened to close, so she stopped talking.

Nate shuffled his feet, then coughed. "He didn't go home, so I'll see him at the Turner's soon, and be sure to tell him."

Scarlett thought she'd misheard. "He stayed there —overnight?"

"Yes, once he'd escorted Chad to the hospital, he returned to the Turners." Nate coughed again. "He's obviously considered close enough to the family to warrant it."

"Really?" This didn't make sense. Sam never bad-mouthed

the family, but he'd intimated several times that he wasn't accepted wholeheartedly into the group as much as Chad thought. She had to tell Nate. "I got the feeling from Lexie and Sam that he was tolerated only because he was Chad's best friend."

Nate frowned. "Then I don't understand why he would put himself through spending the night in that tense atmosphere."

"Chad, Lexie, and Sam were all close," Scarlett tried to justify Sam's behavior to herself as well as Nate. "Perhaps he was there for Lexie since her parents don't appear to be the warmest of souls. Maybe he walked over to Chad's parents later. Anyway, I'm sure there's a good reason. Please make sure Sam's okay."

Nate went down the steps before he answered. "I can only ask."

She smiled encouragingly. "That's what friends do even if they can't do anymore."

Placing his cap back on his head, Nate gave a quick nod then headed to his car.

This would undoubtedly make both men uncomfortable, but it could allow Sam to share his feelings about Chad and what had happened. Scarlett was sure that the male members of the secret club wouldn't offer support to an outsider. If only he would get in touch with her. Surely he understood she'd be worried. She'd tried to reach him last night, but his phone went straight to message.

It was frustrating. How could she help if Sam wouldn't talk to her? And why did he feel like he couldn't or didn't want to? Convinced she'd have a message or two from Sam when she woke this morning, those weren't the questions she'd asked herself last night. Instead, she'd only thought of who would want to get Chad out of the picture and why?

Any would have kept her awake, but only one made her stomach twist.

"Don't worry. Even though he doesn't like that kind of thing, Nate will do it for Sam," Violet chattered beside her. Then her eyes widened. "Wait. You're already scheming, aren't you?"

The accusation dragged Scarlett reluctantly back to the present. "Not scheming exactly. After talking to Lexie, I have a strong urge to uncover the truth about the Carver Corporation and this club."

"Why don't we drive to the library and look them up?" Ruby joined them at the door as George ran inside. "There's plenty of information there about Cozy Hollow, important people in its history, and all the places nearby."

Violet groaned. "But it's Sunday, the library's closed."

"Not for the librarian." Ruby plucked up her car keys and dangled them from the large brass one attached to a sturdy ring. "I have the power."

Without hesitation, Scarlett headed to the bedroom to collect her bag. "Let's go."

"Not so fast," Violet called out. "Some of us need breakfast."

Violet's stomach usually came first—but not today.

"Grab some fruit," she said over her shoulder.

"We can make toast there," Ruby suggested when Violet stomped down the hall.

Muttering came from Violet's room, and Scarlett wasn't above using bribery. "To make up for it, I'll make a lovely lunch when we get home."

Violet capitulated ungracefully. "I'm holding you to that."

Ruby quickly fed Bob and George, and soon they traipsed out the front door with the pets following at their heels. It was going to be an impromptu family outing, and Scarlett didn't mind in the least. The pets were great travelers who hated being left behind and spent every weekday at the library with Ruby. Well, Bob did.

George tended to wander at will around town, visiting the house where he used to live with his previous owner—the now deceased ex-librarian, Mabel Norris, and putting his nose into people's business—literally.

CHAPTER NINE

A dark and somber old building, the library was nestled on Main Street between a quiet walkway and the council building and only two short blocks down from the Cozy Café. A grass area in front of the steps held a bench seat, small fountain, giant tree, and a wide path running along the right of these. The carved doors were impressive and very heavy. Once unlocked, Ruby had to put a bit of effort into pushing one open.

"Why didn't we come in from the back?" Violet glanced around suspiciously.

"We're not doing anything wrong, and I still get a kick coming through that door," Ruby explained unapologetically.

"It doesn't matter which door we use, but let's lock it, so we don't get disturbed." Suddenly jittery, Scarlett took care of this herself.

Once Ruby handed her the key, she turned the lights on. One of the first things she'd done after taking the job was to request funds from the mayor, a personal friend, to have an electrician put in more lights. Now the place was a good deal brighter, which also gave it more warmth.

"Come over to the Cozy Hollow history area." Ruby led the way to the corner opposite her small office.

Behind the shelves of these books was the washroom. It wasn't a large building, yet Ruby had made every nook more inviting with large cushions and comfortable chairs. Scarlett and Violet were proud of their sister in so many ways.

With a grunt, Ruby pulled out a hefty tome, placing it on one of the tables.

"Let's begin with this one." She flipped over the cover to the first page, after the title and acknowledgments. It was a double-spread of sepia pictures, and they leaned down to get a better look.

Violet read the heading. "Fore-fathers of Cozy Hollow and a history of the surrounds."

"That's the Turner and Wood families." Scarlett pointed to the names underneath. "Plus, the Johnsons and Whitleys. I've seen what must be the originals at Lexie's place."

"So, there were four families originally, just like now?" Ruby asked.

"Looks that way. It says they settled here in the 1870s." Scarlett pointed to the paragraph under the heading. Then she pulled out her phone and took pictures of these pages and several more. "We need to find out more about these families."

Scarlett flicked through a few more pages, but there was nothing more relating to the Carver Corporation to pique her interest. "I think we should ask Lexie for more details on what each of these families does in the business."

"Nate will have already asked those questions." Violet pointed out. "Besides, do you really think she'll want to speak to us right now?"

Ruby put the book back on the shelf with an attempted flourish—which failed because of the weight. "Maybe not us, but she likes Scarlett. Otherwise, she wouldn't have spoken so frankly at the wedding."

"With the catering, we've met a few times, but we didn't suddenly become friends," Scarlett stated.

"Since Lexie's a good friend of Sam's, why did you not meet her before?" Violet asked.

The innocent question struck a chord, and Scarlett tried to laugh about it. "I must admit I was concerned that Sam was embarrassed about me. He spent a lot of time with them, but there's always a reason why I'm not invited to their events. Maybe I'm not posh enough."

Her sisters didn't laugh or find it even slightly amusing. Ruby looked shocked, while Violet seemed speculative.

"So she was desperate enough to have your services, but after Chad's death, why did she bother to speak to you at all?" Violet demanded.

This was yet another thing Scarlett thought about last night. "I'm not sure, but I do know that being traumatized can affect people in all sorts of ways. Maybe I was the right or only person when she needed someone to vent to."

Ruby smiled. "That doesn't mean she didn't appreciate you being there for her."

Scarlett nodded. "I'll ask her to meet with me tomorrow. It's worth the chance she may say yes."

"I bet she'll jump at any chance to get away from home. Her parents didn't look the types to spend hours commiserating," Violet said dryly.

Ruby's mouth trembled. "How awful to have to deal with this on her own."

Scarlett's phone rang at that moment, and she was relieved on several counts, mainly because Sam's number was showing as the caller. "How are you doing," she asked gently.

"I've been better." The pause was lengthy. "Ah, Scarlett, this is a little awkward, but I need a favor."

It was awkward, but she heard in his voice how hard it was for him to ask. "Anything I can do, you know I'll try."

"Sure. Ah, would you come to the Turners and stay with Lexie for a while? Her parents and the business partners are having a meeting at the factory, and she'll be alone, which I don't think is a great idea right now."

He sounded nervous. Perhaps Lexie was unstable, but Scarlett wasn't convinced she should be the one to take care of an almost stranger. "I don't understand why she'd ask for me. How come you won't be there?"

"I don't want to leave her, but I need to get some clean clothes, and I have a meeting with my boss. It shouldn't take me too long, but if it's too much trouble. . ?"

She didn't like the way he phrased this, but with what he was going through, decided to give him the benefit of the doubt. "I'll be there soon."

"Thank you. I appreciate this."

Then he was gone, and she stared at the phone as if it might explain his manner. When she looked up, it was to find her sisters watching her. Reluctantly Scarlett told them what he wanted.

"Wow, it may be odd, but you have to admit that it's perfect timing," Ruby said.

"Do you want us to come?" Violet asked.

Scarlett shook her head. "Too many people might be a little much for her, and she'd probably not be as open."

"But before you go, I do have one question," Violet arms were crossed, and her foot tapped in that way she had. "What happened to my lunch?"

Sheepishly, Scarlett wrapped her in a hug. "You don't really mind, do you?"

Violet sniffed. "Save the sugar for Lexie and Sam."

Ruby led them to the front door. "I'll make us something, Vi."

Then they called the pets, and Scarlett dropped them off home, fully aware that her sisters were dying to have more of a conversation about Sam's behavior.

* * *

As soon as she arrived at the Turners, Sam ran out to the van and opened her door. "Sorry that call was so abrupt and that I didn't say goodbye properly yesterday. I'm all over the place at the moment."

Dark circles around his eyes and bristles on his usually clean-shaven cheeks spoke volumes. Scarlett got out and kissed his cheek. "Don't apologize. It's a terrible time for you, and I don't expect you to worry about me."

He let out a sigh. "Thanks for understanding. The truth is that Lexie's blaming herself, and I don't think it wise to leave her alone. Her parents seem oblivious and haven't given her more than a few minutes of compassion." His eyes flashed, and his hands clenched into fists. "Consoling Chad's mom takes precedence."

Scarlett had never seen him this angry. The way he spat the words out was a little frightening. Hoping to soothe him, she rubbed a hand along his upper arm. "Then I'm glad I came. As long as Lexie doesn't mind me being here, take as long as you need. There's nothing urgent I need to get home for."

He smiled and headed to the front door. "I've told Lexie you're coming. It's hard to say if she took it in or not, but I do know that she likes you." His face darkened once more. "I don't know why her mom couldn't have stayed. Then again, she probably wouldn't have made Lexie feel any better."

He sounded so bitter, and Scarlett didn't know what to say, so she remained silent as they went straight to the conservatory. Lexie sat with her fingers in the small pond, waving them back and forward in a mesmerizing way.

As they neared her, Sam called softly, "Lexie? Scarlett's here."

Lexie looked up to stare at them blankly.

"She's going to be with you while I go home and tidy up and talk to my boss," Sam continued.

Lexie's eyes widened in horror, and her mouth quivered. "Don't go. There are plenty of clothes here."

Sam flinched, yet his voice was gentle. "Sorry, Sweetie. We talked about this—I'm not wearing Chad's clothes."

Scarlett gasped. How had that suggestion even arisen?

"No, I guess that wouldn't be right." Lexie gulped. "What shall I do with them? His bag is right there in the hall cupboard—ready for our honeymoon."

Certain that hysteria was close to the surface for the poor woman, Scarlett leaned in close to Sam. "Can I talk to you in the hall?"

Hesitating for a moment, he eventually nodded. Scarlett told him what she thought of Lexie's condition when they got out of earshot and sight. "This is not normal. I think Lexie's taken or been given something."

Sam merely nodded. "The doctor came late last night. At her mom's insistence, he gave Lexie something to calm her." He turned back to the room. "She was sobbing most of the night, so it wasn't the worst idea. Then, Mrs. Turner forced her to take more this morning. I'll make sure that's the last of it."

It was sweet how determined Sam was to take care of Lexie, but with these mood swings, it was clear that he struggled almost as much. "I'm glad. Drugs will only delay her ability to deal with Chad's death. You look exhausted. Why don't you take a nap before you come back?"

He sighed heavily. "If I thought I could sleep, I'd take your advice, but I'm so worried about Lexie that it's impossible to close my eyes."

"You're a good friend, Sam," she said softly.

He paled and backed away as if she'd said something hurtful. "Not as good as I could have been. I'd better go, and I'll hurry."

Poor Sam was as tied in knots over this with guilt as Lexie, and as much as she hated drugs, perhaps he would benefit by a sleeping pill for one night. She'd suggest it when he got back.

Heading back inside the conservatory, she sat beside Lexie on the edge of the pond. Unable to bring herself to ask questions, after a minute or two, with no prompting, Lexie began to ramble.

"The sheriff came for a little while. He was kind, but he asked so many questions, and Sam made him leave. I want to, but we can't help with the investigation."

Scarlett tutted. "That's a shame."

"There's a lot I don't know," Lexie continued as if Scarlett hadn't spoken. "Chad was a good man. The best."

"I didn't know him well, but he seemed to be," Scarlett agreed.

"Everyone loved him."

Clearly, not everyone, otherwise he wouldn't be dead. Scarlett shook her head at that dark thought. Lexie should be encouraged to talk, but maybe some fresh air would be good for both of them. "Would you like to go for a walk outside?"

"I would," Lexie managed before her mouth trembled again. "Not to the beach!"

"Absolutely not. How about around this side of the house? Since I haven't been out this way, you can show me around."

"Okay." Lexie stood and wavered for a moment. "We can use this door. It's closer."

Scarlett hadn't seen the door at the far end of the conservatory yesterday and taking Lexie's arm in case she stumbled in her grogginess, they went outside to a different vista than she'd imagined. Surprisingly, they were in a walled garden. A massive redwood dominated one corner. Shrubs cut into perfect shapes were dotted evenly across the lawn, which hadn't a twig or blade of grass out of place.

Starting at the glass door, they slowly followed the house in a slight curve. It took several minutes, and when the conservatory's large windows ended, the house continued until the uniform bricks were broken by two sturdy doors that were at right-angles to each other in the corner.

Lexie stopped and looked around them as if seeing this aspect for the first time. "My life is exactly this—a walled garden. The only time I'm allowed out is to be put on show or perform some duty. I haven't been free since I came home from college. I'm always watched."

Scarlett assumed she meant she had a body-guard, which sounded so alien, even in her head that she glossed over that to concentrate on the freedom aspect. "You can't mean that literally. As an adult, surely you can go anywhere you choose?"

"Not unless I'm prepared to listen to my parents tell me the errors of my ways. Hah!" Lexie's laugh was ugly. "That's putting it nicely. Let me tell you that those arguments are like nothing you can imagine."

Scarlett's stomach clenched. She'd had a taste of Mrs. Turner's displeasure and seen her husband's directed at others. If Lexie was to be believed, then these were obviously mild doses. "So that's why you agreed to marry Chad?"

"I had no choice." Lexie shuddered. "It could have been a lot worse."

Scarlett filed that away. "But you didn't love Chad."

Lexie shook her head sadly. "And you've probably heard

that he didn't love me. We both wanted other people." Glancing at Scarlett, she quickly looked away.

"Did these other people want to marry you and Chad?"

"Possibly. Neither of us chose to go down that track because it was useless to discuss it." Her words were clipped and dismissive.

Scarlett stopped short of asking who she was referring to. Maybe later she could bring it up because right now she was sure that she wouldn't get an answer. Or perhaps she didn't want to know. "You must have loved that man very much?"

Lexie nodded, her head downcast. "I might seem like a stupid woman, but I do appreciate that finding out who killed Chad is difficult with all these secrets."

Scarlett nodded. "It is hard, but no one thinks you're stupid."

"I beg to differ. There are plenty around here who expect me to behave like a good child," Lexie scoffed. "The sad thing is that Chad might still be here if I had stood up for myself."

"You don't know that for certain. Besides, the sheriff is talking to everyone again today. He'll find the killer." Scarlett put one hand behind her back to hide the crossed fingers.

"I hope so and that it's soon. Sam and I won't be able to move forward until that happens," Lexie's voice wobbled. "I badly wanted to help, but I hardly paid attention to who was here, and I didn't see the guest list. The cake was my only real contribution."

Lexie's story was all kinds of tragic, but Sam's name thrown in there so casually made things awkward again. Scarlett focused once more on the sham of the wedding.

"You looked so happy yesterday. It's hard to believe you were so against the marriage."

Lexie lifted her head and grimaced. "There were many people who expected me to play the delighted bride—my parents especially. After all, I was getting the cream of avail-

73

able men they deemed eligible. It's amazing how a couple of stiff whiskeys can help a person keep up appearances."

Scarlett's shock was hard to hide. "You didn't look drunk."

"My family drinks whiskey daily. It would take a good deal more than that to make me drunk. Taking the edge off was a help, and you have to admit it was a lovely day. Until . . ." Lexie gave a shuddering sigh.

"I guess you and Chad would have tried to make each other happy. And you were both escaping, weren't you?" Scarlett suggested.

Lexie lifted her head to stare intently at her. "You're smart —just as Sam said. Chad and I understood that the wedding meant saying goodbye to the lives we really wanted. I never had a shot at that, but Chad thought he could change his parent's minds. Even up until that last week. It nearly broke him, and we talked about going through with it, then divorcing soon after. Our families are so intertwined that everything around us would be affected, so it was merely wishful thinking. Living in a small community like Harmony Beach means that it's easy to upset and disappoint people. Suddenly, time ran out, and every second of that day was a pain he couldn't hide."

That had been so apparent that Scarlett's family had all remarked on the groom's behavior. Therefore, others must have noticed it as well.

"You mentioned a lot of people would be upset, but you have no siblings, and Chad has only one brother. Surely you weren't concerned about other residents, so are there other extended family members to consider?" Scarlett gambled that Lexie was ready to tell her more, and she wasn't disappointed.

"There are. Come, I'll show you." Lexie led the way to one of the heavily carved doors.

She seemed surer of herself as if the drug was wearing

off. Punching numbers on the keypad, mindful not to let Scarlett see, there was a beep, then Lexie pushed the door. It opened slowly but effortlessly.

"It must be electric."

Lexie ignored the statement and moved down a well-lit hall to another door. This one was steel, and again she punched in a code. Inside was a room like no other. A large table with eight chairs, all carved, sat in the middle. Four had very high backs. One wall was covered in bookshelves, another portraits. The back wall had another door, and to the left-hand side of this was a computer and other office equipment. On the right, a high cabinet held goblets and glass decanters filled with amber or red liquid.

"This is a lovely room, but doesn't your father's company have offices in town?"

"That is for business meetings. This is where the board meets when they are discussing the family." Lexie stood by the portraits, pointing to a very old one done in sepia. "These four men began the Carver Corporation and are the reason we are all so wealthy."

Scarlett immediately recognized the picture. It was the same one in the library book and on the study wall. Not wishing to stop Lexie mid-flow, she kept that to herself. "Are they brothers?"

"Not in the traditional sense." Using a fingertip, Lexie traced one of the faces. "They grew up together in a Russian small-town. In the 1870's, when civil unrest became unbearable, they escaped persecution. When they eventually arrived in America, they made their way to Oregon. Apprentice carpenters when they came, they were apparently better than any others in the business and much sought after. Their combined skills encouraged them to make a pact to work together and start their own company. They handed down their talents to the next generation only, sharing their knowledge of forestry as well but never to outsiders. Money was made, and the rest is history."

It sounded like a recitation, and something a young child had been forced to learn. Scarlett moved onto the next picture. In this one, there were eight men.

Lexie followed closely. "That's the original fathers and their sons."

There were another two frames, as there were in the library, suggesting that these were the next generations. The last frame was of seven men. Scarlett recognized Mr. Turner and Mr. Wood—and Chad.

After a few moments, she realized why this one picture was so different.

Lexie laughed dryly at Scarlett's expression. "Yes, you know what this means. I was supposed to be a boy. Imagine what a disappointment I was to my father. Maybe she thinks I'll forget because Mom mentions it often. Due to this little error in genetics, which is somehow my fault, I had to marry Chad to keep the balance of power with my father. With all their careful planning, they didn't foresee this happening," Lexie laughed again.

Scarlett cringed at the unpleasant sound. "How would that keep the power with your family, if Chad was a Wood?"

"It turned out to be simple, but you can imagine the uproar when my father suggested that Chad take my name." Lexie snorted. "Apparently, when it suits, rules can be broken."

The bitterness sapped Lexie's beauty and made Scarlett shiver. "What will happen now?"

All color left Lexie's cheeks. "I don't yet know who, but I will have to marry one of them." She pointed to that last picture.

Scarlett got as close as she could, and she recognized

some faces, but there were no names beneath these originals. "Who are the other men?"

"David Johnson and Joshua Whitley. And we shouldn't discount Chad's brother, Michael. He's not in the picture, because as the youngest son, there was no place for him. Until now."

The disgust was clear and strong. Scarlett's eyes locked on the picture. The faces were staunch and hard, apart from Chad's. Knowing all of them so well, as Lexie must, it would undoubtedly be hard to marry any of them.

The faint sound of voices came from the internal door, and Lexie gasped. "They're back! Quick we have to go."

CHAPTER TEN

They made it outside without being caught. Lexie had a hand to her chest, which rose and fell rapidly. "Forget about that room," she huffed when they reached a large shrub. "I shouldn't have taken you there."

Scarlett looked back at the locked door and the one adjacent. "Why did you? The pictures are the same in the library apart from that last one, so anyone could find out most of the information you just shared."

"I wanted—I needed you to see how it is. To see what they are." Lexie chewed her bottom lip. "Maybe that was a mistake."

It troubled Scarlett that Lexie was pulling her into this mystery with an agenda she didn't fully understand. Was it just to catch a killer, or something more? "I'm glad that you trusted me, but I get the feeling that you didn't tell the sheriff about this?"

Lexie looked down at the grass, but Scarlett couldn't let it go.

"Tell me why you didn't. What do you think I can do about this that Nate can't?"

"I feel so bad about Chad, and you seem to understand."

It sounded too convenient. Lexie's guilt was almost tangible, but there had to be another reason. A more important one.

"You do want the sheriff to catch the killer?"

Lexie's eyes misted. "How can you ask that? I want that more than anything."

She was so earnest that this had to be the truth unless Lexie was a superb actor.

"Then you have to tell him everything. Someone at the wedding knows more than they're admitting. Maybe more than one person."

Lexie stared at the door before grabbing Scarlett's arm. They walked quickly back to the conservatory. Her voice lowered, "I'll talk to the sheriff, but not here. I'll meet you in town. Wait for my call. You should go now."

Scarlett would be happy to leave, but she'd made a promise. "Sam asked me to wait until he got back."

Lexie shook her head firmly and gave Scarlett a small push. "There's no need. My parents are at home. If they weren't in a hospitable mood before, they'll be worse now. Trust me."

It sounded like such a simple request, yet Scarlet wavered back and forth between wanting to get away from here as fast as she could, and not wanting Lexie to endure alone any more tactlessness or meanness from her parents.

In the end, Lexie's fear of being discovered made Scarlett hurry alongside Lexie back the way they'd come. So many things troubled her, but she couldn't be the cause of this woman being poorly treated.

Going straight to the area where the van was parked, Scarlett was about to get in when Mr. Turner marched out the front door.

"There you are, Lexie. What is Ms. Finch doing here?"

With no attempt to hide his suspicion, he glared at both of them before glancing through the van windows.

"Hello, Mr. Turner. I was collecting a plate that we missed in yesterday's pack-up. It happens quite a lot."

"That doesn't sound very efficient."

He looked pointedly at her empty hands, and Scarlett gulped.

"Thanks for finding it in the kitchen, Lexie. It's one of my Mom's favorites, and I couldn't give up on it. Take care." Scrabbling in her haste to get in the van, she whacked her knee on the steering wheel and bit back a squeal of pain.

With a wave and slight skid on the raked gravel, Scarlett took off down the drive as if the hounds of Baskerville were on her heels. The look on Mr. Turner's face stayed with her most of the journey, convincing her she wasn't too far wrong.

Sitting in the van back in her driveway, Scarlett finally relaxed and dissected what she knew. Four men emigrated from Russia. They pooled their resources to build an empire. The reins were handed down to the eldest son of each family, and Lexie's status was an anomaly that her father hoped to correct by marrying Chad.

By the sound of things, Lexie couldn't be on the board and certainly couldn't join the club, even if she wanted to. It was as though they'd stepped back in time, and women were still chasing the vote. For all her money and privilege, Scarlett wouldn't wish for Lexie's life. It occurred to her that Mrs. Turner might have gone with her husband not so much to console Mrs. Wood, but perhaps to talk over the next option of a groom—Chad's brother.

It was sickening just to think that could happen, but what if it were true?

Scarlett arrived home and parked the van. Running her hands around the steering wheel, she circled back to an important question. Was Lexie's treatment from her parents enough of a motive for murdering Chad? If so, did Sam suspect Lexie, and was he trying to protect her?

She all but leaped off the seat when someone yanked the driver's door open. "Ruby!"

"What are you doing out here? We've been waiting for you."

"I *was* thinking," Scarlett replied tersely. "Right now, I'm trying not to have a heart attack."

"Sorry." Ruby shrugged. "It's just that you were gone a while, and when I saw the van out here, I got worried."

Bob must have heard the voices as he bounded down the front steps across the lawn and onto Scarlett's lap. "Get off, you monster," she laughed despite being squashed behind the wheel.

Ruby took him by the collar and pulled him out. "George slunk around the whole property several times, looking for you."

"I doubt that. He was probably looking for food. Scarlett got out of the van and scratched Bob on his rounded stomach. "We seriously need to cut down on their meals."

"They're not fat," Ruby said indignantly.

"Then let Bob sleep on your bed for a change."

"Hah! You know he's decided to be your dog. And never mind your attempts to change the subject, how's Lexie?"

"There's so much more to her than I first thought." Scarlett put her arm through the crook of Ruby's, and they went to the kitchen where Violet was folding washing.

While Ruby made coffee Scarlett told them about the four families and their arrival in America.

"That would be around the time of the pogroms," Ruby elaborated. "There was a lot of unrest in Russia. Burning of towns happened often, and innocent people got caught in the middle, so many became homeless. With little money or food, young men left the country in groups to find a better life. If they had a skill and weren't afraid of hard work, getting jobs was easy. Forestry has always been a steady and profitable business, and they must have been good because Carver Corporation is one of the biggest in Oregon."

Scarlett was never surprised by Ruby's vast knowledge. A bookworm from early on, her sister loved history in particular.

"I wondered where the name originated. I assumed it was an ancestor of Mr. Turner's, but it must be named for the profession," Violet mused.

Scarlett nodded. "That makes sense. You'd love the board-room, Ruby. I didn't get the chance to look at the books, but there were so many it would take years to read them."

"That sounds wonderful." Ruby sighed. "Maybe Lexie will let me see it one day?"

"I wouldn't hold your breath. Lexie only took me there because we were alone and nearly had kittens when she heard someone in the house. Imagine being so scared of your parents."

Ruby shook her head. "I know it happens, but I can't get my head around it."

"That's bad enough," Violet retorted. "But what about having no choice of husband, and having to sit by while the men around you have everything their own way?"

"Arranged marriages happen all around the world; it's the way she's treated that annoys me most." Scarlett took a long drink. "You'd think that going along with what her parents wanted should give her some kind of kudos. Her new husband, who is also her close friend, is killed, and she's given no sympathy or support."

Ruby sniffed, and Scarlett took her hand. "You said earlier that you're friends with Ellen?"

"We haven't spoken in a while before the wedding, and I hardly saw her yesterday."

That was disappointing, yet Scarlett didn't want to let the connection go. "Lexie said she'd call me some time, but I don't want to wait, and we're all working tomorrow. Would you mind calling Ellen and ask if she'd like to come by for supper?"

"If you think it might help, I will, but Nate was going to see her today." Ruby reminded her.

"A different perspective can't hurt, right?"

"I guess not." Ruby shrugged. "I'll do it now."

She took the phone into the hall and returned before long with a smile. Ellen was pleased to hear from me and said she'd love to catch up."

"Maybe her household isn't harmonious either," Violet suggested.

Having taken note of the reactions at the wedding, Scarlett didn't doubt that was the case.

CHAPTER ELEVEN

As promised, Scarlett cooked supper. The pie was perfect, thanks to the recent purchase of a new oven. A medley of vegetables accompanied it, and dessert was a cream sponge with strawberries.

Ellen arrived with a fancy bottle of wine and was effusive at seeing her school friend and kissed Ruby's cheek. "It's been forever if you don't count the wedding."

Violet and Scarlett waited at the end of the hall and backed away so that the others could enter the kitchen.

Ruby introduced her. "I'm so glad you could come on short notice."

"I have to be honest; I was desperate to get away from my family. It's wonderful to catch up with you again, despite the horrific circumstances." Ellen's lip quivered but she seemed determined not to cry.

"I guess Harmony Beach is a difficult place to be at the moment, with so much confusion about what happened yesterday," Scarlett commented.

"You have no idea." Ellen pursed her lips. "The whole area

is rife with conjecture, and everyone wants to have their say. Having the sheriff around so much isn't helping either."

Violet opened the wine while rolling her eyes at Scarlett.

Ellen's priorities did seem a little skewed. Were all of the families at Harmony Beach like this? Scarlett wondered as she brought the food to the table. "Please take a seat."

"This looks delicious!" Ellen said excitedly. "We don't have anything like this at home. You know, it takes me back to college days and eating in the cafeteria."

Ruby giggled nervously. Violet smirked, and Scarlett tried not to choke on her wine. Ellen might mean it as a compliment, but Ruby had commented more than once that the food at college wasn't of a high standard. Scarlett was confident that her food was several levels above that, but none of them corrected their guest.

After drinking her wine quickly and happy to have another, Ellen became a talker and didn't need much encouragement to describe her life. It was quite different from Lexie's and nothing remotely like the way the Finch sisters lived theirs.

When there was a slight pause, Violet, in her usual manner, jumped in with both feet. "Are you involved with anyone?"

Ellen dabbed at the corners of her mouth with a napkin. "I wish. Eligible men are as scarce as hen's teeth around here. Although I'm thinking of traveling, which might help change that."

"Will you travel with Rebecca?" Ruby asked.

"Gosh, no!" Ellen grimaced. "We haven't seen eye-to-eye for a while now."

"That sounds bad," Violet teased, one eye on Scarlett.

Ellen shrugged. "Not really. When you live and breathe our parent's company, seeing the same people all the time wears you down. It's as though there are no new conversations—just a re-hashing of old ones. We still see each other, and we're okay with that, but we don't hang out unless necessary."

"But you were so close," Ruby protested.

"It might have seemed that way to outsiders. Now that we're older and out of school, we don't have to pretend." Ellen smiled as if this were completely normal.

"I'm not sure I understand why you had to pretend to be friends," Scarlett said casually.

Ellen carefully put her knife and fork down and sat back in her chair to study them one at a time. "I don't mean to be rude, but you're asking a lot of questions. It feels like I'm being grilled."

Ruby twisted her hands. "I'm sorry, Ellen. We . . ."

"It's my fault," Scarlett interrupted. "I asked Ruby to invite you here tonight. We're concerned for Lexie and hoped that you could help us understand what happened. Maybe between us, we could help her."

"How sweet you are to worry. Ruby's always been a mother hen, but after all, you barely know Lexie." Ellen's smile was strained. "Don't trouble yourself too much—Lexie's family will take care of her."

"Perhaps you're not aware that I'm Sam's girlfriend, and he's worried sick about her," Scarlett explained. "We'd very much like to do something."

"I can see caring runs in the family, and I did hear that Sam had a girlfriend. Still, her family wouldn't accept an outsider's involvement, no matter how well-intentioned." Ellen took a long drink of her wine. "That's just the way our parents are. I also suspect nothing, but the sheriff finding the killer will make a difference to Lexie."

Scarlett nodded, although she found this attitude frustrating. "Maybe so, but do you know any reason why someone would want to kill Chad?"

Ellen didn't hesitate, "Jealousy."

Violet's fork stopped midway to her mouth. "Who was jealous?"

"There are plenty of people at Harmony Beach and in the surrounding areas who think our families have too much." Ellen's voice was full of disdain.

Violet ignored Scarlett's warning glance to back off.

"Men or women?"

"Take your pick. Good-looking and rich—that's all people need to be jealous." Ellen abruptly stood, her chair almost toppling. "Suddenly I've lost my appetite for this home-made fare. When all this blows over, give me a call, Ruby. And let's meet somewhere else."

No one protested as she swept up her bag and marched down the hall. Ruby did follow, apologizing repeatedly.

"Do you think she meant people were jealous of Chad or Lexie?" Violet tapped the table with a fingernail. "They were both good-looking and rich, but I suspect she had someone in particular in mind and couldn't bring herself to say who it is."

"I think you're right, and she was annoyed that we didn't pick up on who she meant. Frankly, there's too many to choose from when we know so little about most of them. It has occurred to me that following in his father's footsteps, Chad was next in line to be the Chairperson of the board. And if Lexie couldn't be CEO like her father, maybe Chad would fill that position too." Scarlett stood and paced the kitchen. "That must be frustrating for the rest of that generation.

Bob joined her, his nails clicking on the tiled floor in time to Violet's tapping.

Scarlett stopped when Ruby came back a little distraught.

"I tried to take her keys and let me call a taxi, but she wouldn't listen. I hope she's okay to drive."

"I'm sure you did your best. Ellen looked like she could handle her drink and she did eat," Scarlett assured her and since they could do no more she changed the subject. "Do you know if it's possible to hold both the CEO and chairman positions?"

Ruby shook her head. "I don't think so. If I'm not mistaken, it would be a conflict of interest."

"Right." Scarlett tried to picture the hierarchy as it might be. "So who would fill the Chairperson's position if Chad became the CEO?"

"One of the other sons?" Violet suggested. "Chad has a brother, Michael."

"That's a point. I imagine that would be a particularly unpleasant proposition for Lexie. It appears that the whole board changes with each generation because I saw no older men in those later pictures who sat in the high-back chairs. Which makes me think the likely candidate will be another son of the four families. That said, we may have missed someone who'd fit the criteria."

Ruby chewed her bottom lip. "We should find out what their rules are so we can make better assumptions."

"Ellen's hints make things even more intriguing." Violet raised a finger at her sisters. "Don't look at me like that. I meant that we can now match faces to suspects, right?"

"True," Scarlett admitted, "but it also means that there are far too many suspects. I hope Lexie calls me soon. As much as she makes it sound like she isn't privy to much of what goes on, the way Lexie led me to that room makes me think that she knows more than she wants to admit."

"What about Sam?" Violet asked. "As Chad's best friend, he'd have to know plenty about the family."

"He hasn't contacted me." Scarlett felt a pang. "I've left

messages, but he's probably busy at work, or it could be that he's helping with the funeral arrangements."

Violet tutted. "Do you honestly think the Turners or the Johnsons will let him be involved?"

Scarlett crouched to pat Bob who'd begun to whine at her unrest. "That's a valid point. Sam's tolerated because of his relationship with Chad. Wouldn't it be awful if they decided to exclude him from everything?"

Violet nodded. "He seems determined to be allowed to hang around Lexie, so it can't be that bad. Are you going to talk to Nate about any of this?"

"Definitely." Scarlett screwed up her nose. "He won't be happy about us meddling."

"He'll get over it when he finds out about the great information we can share."

Scarlett wasn't as convinced of this as Violet. "After spending all night and today questioning people, don't you think he'll know all this already?"

"Maybe. But you have a way of getting people to say things they wouldn't normally to a sheriff."

"Why, Violet, I'm taking that as a compliment."

"Don't get a big head over it. How was Ellen when she left?"

Ruby instantly looked sad. "Ellen wasn't impressed despite enjoying her meal. She said she could have had the same conversation at home and expected more of me. That wasn't the woman I went to college with, but I guess we've both changed, and she's had a tough time recently."

Scarlett tutted and hugged her. As far as she was concerned, Ruby had also gone through her share of troubles and managed to stay the same sweet person she'd always been. "I guess we could have been more upfront about the reason for the invite, but I don't think she would have come."

"Probably not," Ruby agreed morosely. "I hope she'll forgive me."

"Please, no one ever stays mad with you." Violet smirked.

Scarlett shook her head. "Two compliments in a few minutes? Okay, what have you done with our sister?"

Violet rolled her eyes.

CHAPTER TWELVE

The café was a welcome sight. Mornings surrounded by the smells of fresh baking and familiar sounds relaxed Scarlett more than anything else could. It was her home away from home, and she loved it as much if not more than the family home.

Violet was making chicken soup from scratch, and Scarlett had just placed blueberry muffins in the oven when Nate appeared at the kitchen door.

He took off his hat and came inside with an official air about him. "I hear you've been talking to Ellen Whitley?"

Putting her mixing bowl in the large sink, Scarlett tried for nonchalance. "She stopped by last night."

"Hmmm. Ellen said, you asked her a lot of questions."

"We did discuss her family dynamics. And Lexie's."

"Why would you do that when I specifically asked you not to interfere?"

Violet brushed passed him to wash cookie dough off her hands and make coffee, and Scarlett offered him a seat.

Nate sat with ill-grace. "I guess that means you know more than you got from Ellen."

To give her a little time, Scarlett placed cookie trays in the oven then sat opposite him. "Lexie asked me to visit her yesterday. She showed me a private room hidden in plain sight behind a blank brick wall outside the conservatory."

Nate leaned forward and pulled out his notebook and pen, quickly flicking to a new page. "Go on."

"Essentially, it's a boardroom and is set up with eight chairs around a table. There are photos of the four families who run the Carver's Corporation. Ellen's family is one of them. Lexie's is another."

"The business and who runs it isn't a secret," he stated.

Scarlett nodded. "It's well documented in the library. But have you any idea how these families decide who runs the company? It's all hereditary, and only men can do so. Women aren't allowed."

She heard the outrage in her voice, and Nate grimaced. "It's old-fashioned, I agree, but not exactly rare or illegal. Was it Ellen who told you this?"

"No, it was Lexie. She wasn't happy about it."

"That doesn't make her the killer."

Scarlett shook her head. "I didn't mean that. I believe her when she says she loved Chad. Only, she admitted that it wasn't the right kind of love. Don't you think it's fair to say that there would be others within this group who know how they truly felt about each other?"

"Maybe, but she put on a good show of pretending they were more than friends, even on her wedding day, which you're suggesting she didn't want. Often we're told what we want to hear. Weeding out the truth from what suspects say is not always easy, but it is part of my job," he finished wryly.

"She had no choice to put on a show, and Sam could tell you that she'd been plied with drugs before and since to make everything palatable," Scarlett argued.

Violet placed hot coffee in front of them. "We all know that people tell Scarlett things that they won't say to the law."

He blew on the steaming liquid. "Is that so?"

"You know darn well it is," Violet scoffed. "And what she doesn't hear, Ruby does."

"I do not deny that your sisters are very approachable. Even so, I don't want any of you harassing everybody."

It stuck out like an unfrosted cupcake that he'd just insinuated that Violet wasn't so easy going, and Nate's cheeks were flushed as if he already regretted his statement.

Scarlett was annoyed by his lack of tact. "I can't help it if people call me. And it's certainly not our fault that the café and library are natural places to congregate to discuss things."

"I think you mean to glean information." Nate stood and plucked his hat from the stand near the door. "Tell them to call me instead."

Violet made a disgusted sound and left to attend a customer.

The tenuous relationship between Violet and Nate now appeared to be broken, and despite the sheriff being occasionally officious, Scarlett was genuinely sorry about that. "Will you go see Rebecca?"

"She's on my list to revisit, but it's a mighty big list," he ended on a sigh.

At that moment, Scarlett really looked at him. White lines stood out around his mouth, and there was darkness under his eyes. How had they gone unnoticed? "Are you okay, Nate?"

His eyebrows shot up. "Why do you ask?"

"You look tired."

He ran fingers through his hair and had a pained expression. "When an investigation has so many people involved, there's a lot of pressure to put the case to bed as quickly as possible. Ironically, that means we don't see our bed as much as we like. Especially when certain people withhold evidence."

She flinched. "It's never intentional, and as it happens as I left Lexie's place yesterday, she said she'd be in touch." Before he could tell her off again, she added, "I promise, I did hear you about sending people your way, but Lexie needs a friend right now. I won't turn her down if she asks to see me again."

Nate sighed again. "Just don't go off on a tangent without telling me."

"I won't." She smiled tentatively. "I'm sorry to nag, but I do think you need to look at the book in the library to understand the background of this club. To me, it sounds sinister, which I admit could be because of what's happened."

There was a long pause before he nodded. "You do have an active imagination, but I'll look into it."

"I promise you'll find it interesting at the very least. And please take care of yourself."

Finally, he gave a wry smile. "I'll do my best."

When he'd gone, Violet came back into the kitchen as if she'd been waiting for him to leave. "Just when I think we're getting on fine, I want to kick his shins."

Scarlett chuckled. "I think you have a similar effect on him."

Violet shrugged. "Maybe, but I don't like being bossed around. Not even by a sheriff."

"Does anyone? Although he does deserve for us to at least try to heed him, then he might be more forgiving. And perhaps he wouldn't be like that in a relationship."

"Trust me, he would," Violet argued. "In the short time we were an item, I could see that he was incapable of separating himself from being a sheriff."

"I'm sure it is difficult, but I do like him, and he still likes you."

Scarlett thought she was being diplomatic, but Violet glared.

"We've been over this a hundred times. I don't dislike him, most of the time, but I have no romantic interest in Nate at all. And it wouldn't bother me in the slightest if you did."

"Pardon? Me?" Scarlett gave a brittle laugh. "All I said was that he's a nice guy doing his job, and I think you should cut him a little slack. How does that translate into I like him romantically?"

Violet rolled her eyes but didn't argue. Her sister was hot-headed but not totally unreasonable. Perhaps taking the attitude that attack was the best defense was an attempt to make Scarlett keep her opinions to herself. All she wanted was Violet and Nate; if they genuinely couldn't work things out between them, to find a way to be the friends they once were.

A cacophony from the café scattered her thoughts, as the regular knitting club ladies descended. It would likely take all their wits to keep up with their questions, and Reba Fuller didn't bother with pleasantries as Violet placed cups in front of them.

"So, who do you think did it?"

"I've got no idea. Coffee?" Scarlett held up the pot.

"Well, you surely know." Reba barely took a breath. "The sheriff must have shared something."

"And why would he do that? It's not like we're a couple."

Only Violet's voice gave a clue that she was more than a little annoyed, but Reba was either oblivious or didn't care.

"What? When did you break up?"

Collen nudged her friend's arm. "I told you all about it."

"I think I'd remember something like that," Reba replied haughtily.

Colleen sniffed. "You can't even remember what you're knitting half the time."

The others laughed, while the indignant Reba held out her cup to Scarlett. "I suppose we may as well have a bite to eat. Anything new from the kitchen today?"

"We've got some fresh strawberry tarts. And Violet's making chicken soup which you could take home for supper."

Reba nodded. "Yes, to both."

Collen smacked her lips together. "They sound perfect. I'll have the same."

Violet took the orders then headed out to the kitchen with Scarlett.

"Nice work. I was worried they'd never order once they got started playing twenty questions."

Scarlett grinned. "Lucky for you, they love our food. Otherwise, you could have been stuck out there for hours."

"Days even." Violet laughed dryly as she checked the soup.

CHAPTER THIRTEEN

That afternoon, just as Scarlett and Violet were about to close the café, Lexie swept in the open back door like a princess. She wore a fitted dress that flowed around her ankles, and her golden hair swung around her pretty face. It wasn't until she got closer that they saw how red-rimmed her eyes were as they darted around the kitchen, and that her barely-there smile seemed brittle.

"Come in." Scarlett smiled encouragingly. "We're just finishing up for the day, but please take a seat."

"It smells so good in here." Lexie peered out the window, then into the café before sitting at the table, talking all the while. "I hope you don't mind me coming unannounced. It's difficult to get away right now, so I decided on the spur of the moment when the opportunity presented itself. It's a perfect day for a drive, and the town is so pretty right now." Lexie opened and shut the clasp on her bag several times.

Scarlett covered the dainty hands with her own, temporarily stopping the habit. "Are you okay? You seem nervous."

Lexie stared at their hands and gulped. "I can't shake the

99

feeling I'm being watched. I should be used to it, but this feels different."

Violet had been sweeping. Now she placed the broom against the counter, which slipped and thudded onto the floor, making the other's jump. "Why would someone watch you?"

Lexie licked her lips. "According to my father, there are a ton of reasons."

"Like?" asked Violet.

"Kidnapping. Extortion." Lexie shrugged. "My family is quite wealthy."

"I thought as much, what with the house, fancy cars, and clothes," Violet noted wryly.

Lexie blushed. "I wasn't showing off. Apparently, these things attract the low-life's."

Scarlett shook her head at her sister to warn her from commenting that this was obvious.

Violet sat on the other side of Lexie. "I was teasing."

"Sorry." Lexie grimaced. "Teasing isn't something I under-stand. I'm a bit slow when it comes to reading other people's mannerisms."

Scarlett squeezed Lexie's hands. "Slow is not something I would tag you with, and Ruby said that you did exceptionally well at college."

Lexie nodded shyly. "I do have a degree in business."

"That's wonderful," Scarlett exclaimed, wondering if she'd ever be able to make use of it. "Violet and I had to leave college before we finished."

"Was that to look after your mom?" Lexie gave them a pitying look.

"Yes, did Ruby tell you?"

Lexie shook her head. "Sam explained your situation. He also said that Violet might be going back to college soon. Is that right?"

"It's a little tricky right now," Violet fussed with her apron and eventually took it off. "Once we hire another person, I'll decide what I should or can do."

Lexie nodded, suddenly enthusiastic. "I saw the advertisement for staff a while back. I guess you didn't have any luck with applicants?"

Scarlett saw the same pained expression on Violet's face, which must be mirrored on her own. Not willing to explain the depths of deception their previous employee had used to extort money from them, she offered a watered-down version. "The woman we hired wasn't a good fit."

Lexie pondered that for a moment. "Do you have to be a cook to work here?"

"It helps," Violet laughed.

Lexie looked toward the window again. "That's a shame. I can barely boil water."

"Wait," Violet made a disbelieving sound. "You want a job?"

"Desperately." Since Scarlett had released her hold, Lexie resumed the clasp clicking. "I don't care what it is."

Violet snorted. "I don't think telling a prospective employer you don't care about the job will get you further than a first interview."

Lexie paused. "I shouldn't be honest?"

"There's honesty, and then there's indifference. When you hire someone, you want them to be eager to learn because that means they want to be good at it," Scarlett explained, unsure what to make of the whole conversation. Was Lexie just talking for the sake of it, or did she mean what she was saying?

"That's a good point. The problem is that I don't have any work experience and my father won't let me work in the business. I can't work for a competitor, and no one will hire me anyway because of my family," Lexie clarified.

Violet frowned. "Why would who your family is matter to an employer?"

"My father can be a bit...bullish."

Scarlett leaned forward. As far as she was concerned, Mr. Turner had a lot of say in too many people's lives, but she wanted to hear why an intelligent woman couldn't get a job in her father's company. "Meaning?"

"If my father doesn't like something, because it doesn't meet his exacting standards, the person responsible will know all about it." She blushed. "That tends to scare people off, in case it turns out to be me that's the liability."

"Does that bother you?" Violet pressed.

"Of course it does. I hate that any prospective jobs are lost over who I am rather than what I can do. My parents were proud of my grades, but they made it clear that I was expected to marry and start a family soon after I finished college. I managed to delay things a little, but when I couldn't get work outside of the company, there seemed little point in fighting them." She gulped once more. "Now that Chad's gone, my future looks even bleaker because at least we were friends and respected each other. Who knows how I'll feel about the next candidate, my parents foist on me, but it certainly won't be someone I love. Having no control over my life is soul-destroying, and I've decided that I need to be free to make my own choices." This last bit came out as a whisper.

Just then, Sam came through the open door. His eyes searched the kitchen. "Thank goodness I saw your car as I drove by. I've been looking everywhere for you."

It was abundantly clear that he was referring to Lexie, who looked like she'd been caught doing something wrong. Evidently relieved, Sam hurried to her side and crouched, placing a hand on Lexie's as if touching her was something he had to do.

Awkwardness descended, and Scarlett's skin prickled. "Do you two need some time alone?"

Sam was nodding when his head jerked, and guiltily he met her gaze. "That's not necessary. Now that I know she's okay."

"Why would you think she was in danger?" Scarlett demanded.

Red-faced, Sam slowly stood. "Chad's death wasn't an accident."

"No, but Lexie hasn't been threatened. Has she?" Talking normally, Scarlett watched his every move. His fingers twitched as though he wanted to resume touching Lexie. The prickle turned into a full-blown stabbing to her stomach. How blind she'd been to where Sam's true feelings lay.

Lexie married his best friend, and Sam would have respected that, but there was no way he could have developed the feelings for Lexie, which were now so evident in the last few days.

Also standing, Scarlett took a deep breath, welcoming Violet's move to her side. Together they stared unhappily at the couple before them.

Sam regarded their stance but didn't comment on it. Instead, he spoke as if nothing were amiss between them. It was all about Lexie.

"Lexie believes she's being watched."

Scarlett played along. "So she said. Do you know by whom?"

"I've got a pretty good idea," Sam glared at no one in particular. "Only our sheriff won't listen, and Lexie thinks I'm crazy."

Scarlett crossed her arms. "I'm sure that's not true, but tell us about it anyway."

Sam merely sent Lexie an apologetic glance. "I've been

watching the Johnson brothers for some time. They've always been jealous of Chad and Lexie."

Lexie closed her eyes. "You don't know what you're saying. I've known them all my life, and they would never harm Chad."

"David Johnson is in love with you," Sam forced the words out through gritted teeth.

"That's ridiculous," Lexie scoffed. "His focus, like the rest of them, is on the business."

"I've seen the way he looks at you," Sam growled.

Scarlett twisted her hands. "And how does he look at her?"

"Like he . . ."

Maybe it had something to do with the way Scarlett tapped her foot or how her nostrils flared at his lack of tact, but Sam's certainty faded, and his eyes widened.

"Like she's the woman he really wants?" Scarlett suggested before walking across the room to where her bag hung from the coat rack. "This is very enlightening, but I need to get home."

Sam flinched at her tone. "Right now? I'd like to talk privately with you."

With her head full of cotton wool, Scarlett wasn't in the mood to listen to his excuses. Their relationship was built on a lie, and he could wait until she was ready to listen to his explanations. "Tomorrow *might* be better. I've been up since 4 am and I'm tired."

Lexie pushed back her chair, seemingly unaware of the undercurrent. "I'm so sorry, Scarlett. I didn't mean to hold you up. I need to get home too before my father sends out a search party."

Violet saw them to the door. Sam hesitated, but Scarlett couldn't look at him. It was pretty evident that Sam wouldn't divulge his feelings in front of Lexie, and eventually, he joined Lexie at the bottom of the steps. Violet shut the door and leaned against it, watching as Scarlett fussed with her bag.

Taking the few steps necessary, Violet stood in front of Scarlett and held out her arms.

Leaning into her, Scarlett rested her head against her sister's shoulder and shuddered. "I should have seen it before today."

"You did," Violet murmured.

Scarlett went rigid. "Pardon?"

"You suspected at the very least that Sam had a thing for Lexie," Violet insisted. "I saw it on your face when he spoke of her."

About to tell her sister that she was talking rubbish, Scarlett couldn't form the words. At that moment, the truth of it hit her in the stomach. It was not only physical pain but troubled her thoughts on many levels. Choosing to ignore the chemistry, or at least not think about it too much, made her a fool. Considering how many people knew Sam, there were plenty who potentially witnessed his so-called concern, but did others pick up on how much deeper his feelings were for his best friend's bride?

Suddenly, Lexie's words in the conservatory resonated in Scarlett's head, as they finally struck the chord they should have—Lexie would have preferred Sam to Chad.

"You're right. I saw it and talked myself into believing I was jealous and imagining things. Maybe Chad was in the same boat?" Scarlett winced at the unintentional pun. "But why didn't you say something?"

Violet pushed away so that they could see each other. "Would you have listened to me?"

Scarlett searched inside herself for the truth. "Maybe not. I guess we've all been hiding from our own version of the truth. The attraction between Sam and Lexie must have been on the back burner for years, and she certainly acts on the surface as if nothing's changed. It's the way they look at each other that gave the game away, and I feel like I've been walking around with something covering my eyes until today."

Violet hugged her. "You're not the only one who wanted what they couldn't have. Why do you think they allowed it to be like that?"

"If they'd allowed it to come out before, there would have been major repercussions, and if Chad had seen it, they'd probably lose their friendship. With Chad and Lexie scared to cross Mr. Turner and Mr. Wood and, therefore, the inability to change anything, keeping it to themselves was the top priority and maybe the only option for both of them."

Violet raised an eyebrow. "It's hard to fathom in this day and age that this could happen."

Scarlett agreed, and she was already thinking of the times she had seen Lexie and Sam together, which weren't that many and had probably been deliberate. "What about Lexie? She said she preferred Sam, but does that mean she loves him too?"

Violet tipped her head, and Scarlett saw the truth. Now that the blinkers were removed, there was no disputing that she'd seen the longing in Lexie's face and heard it in her voice.

"Of course she does. She tried to protect Sam by not showing it. She told me so much because she probably felt she couldn't share it with Sam just yet."

Violet watched her closely. "Maybe it was noble, or perhaps she wanted it to come out into the open, but it does beg the question—is Sam guilty of more?"

"I don't want to believe that." In her head, Scarlett had already gone there, but even after the way he'd deceived her, it didn't seem plausible. "Sam's kind and thoughtful. Not once have I seen him angry."

"Love can make people do strange things, and we're not around him every minute. Plus, I don't think it was kind that he led you on."

Scarlett's head drooped. "I can't deal with this right now, Vi. I just want to go home. Ruby will be there soon, and I should get dinner started."

"You're in no emotional state to drive," Violet spoke softly, holding her hand out. "Give me the keys."

Pulling them from her bag, Scarlett dropped them into her sister's palm. Since her hands shook so badly, there was no point in arguing.

CHAPTER FOURTEEN

As early and dark as it was the next morning, it shouldn't have been such a relief to get out of bed, but with sleep being once more elusive, that's exactly how it seemed.

Scarlett hung her head in the shower, letting the water cascade over her with the hope it would be energizing. If only it could wash away the hurt and humiliation that Sam had never loved her in the way she thought.

Dissecting every second they'd spent together, she was no closer to understanding how he thought his actions were fair. Getting her to watch out for Lexie yesterday was pretty low, and when did he imagine was the right time to tell her their relationship was nothing but a farce?

Sam called a couple of times last night, but Scarlett wouldn't speak to him. There was nothing he could say that she wanted to hear. Not yet. Violet had kept the phone beside her, and the coolness in her tone every time she answered made even Scarlett shiver. She didn't want to hurt him, but couldn't deal with apologies when every nerve was raw.

If he hadn't sought her out—pursued her—they wouldn't

be in this situation. Scarlett hadn't been looking for a boyfriend and was happy with her life. Now, she was mortified that he'd only ever considered her as second best.

Ruby looked at her funny last night when she'd explained how she felt. Her youngest sister asked if being embarrassed was worse than being hurt. As if that was the important issue.

Finished in the bathroom, Scarlett dressed slowly, contemplating if Ruby had a valid point. Could the two things be separated?

Bob sat in the doorway, whining when she sighed deeply.

"I'm okay, boy. Just having a wallow. Don't you think I deserve to for a while longer?"

His tail thumped on the floor. George jumped over Bob's large body, sauntered across the room, and lay at her feet.

"What do you guys think about Sam? Should I be mad, sad, or glad?"

George proceeded to wash himself while Bob yawned.

Brushing her hair, Scarlett couldn't help smiling at the animals who'd found their way into this family and their hearts in a very short time.

"I guess it's not as riveting as I thought. But you both liked him, right?"

"Are you talking to the pets?" Violet climbed over Bob. "Let me know if you get an answer because they just stare at me.

Scarlett made a rude face and tied her hair up in a bun. "Even these guys aren't interested in the subject matter."

"That's hardly fair." Violet threw herself on the made bed, knowing that this would offend Scarlett's ordered world. "We listened to you for ages last night. Sam is a pig, and you need to move on. There, are we good?"

"I never said that Sam was a pig. Now, get off my bed. And you can tidy it before you leave."

With her arms behind her head, Violet was in no hurry. "I will if you call Sam later this morning."

"What? Why would I do that?"

"Because you'll be like a bear with a toothache until you clear the air. It's not going to be pleasant near you—which is not good for business, or my digestion. If you don't hate Sam, why not get it over with."

"Of course, I don't hate him, but he's hardly my favorite person. Besides, it's not that easy. I don't know what to say."

Violet groaned. "Let him talk. He's the one who strung you along and made you fall in love with his endearing helpfulness."

"I don't remember saying I love him," Scarlett said automatically.

"Aha! You didn't." Violet scooted to the edge of the bed, messing it even further. "All the things you said last night about this being upsetting, mortifying and embarrassing were true, but not once dear sister, did you say you love him. Not then, or over the last few months."

Hands on hips, Scarlett tapped her foot. "Is playing the devil's advocate supposed to make me feel better, or is it simply to show how clever you are?"

Violet grinned. "Maybe. What it should do is make you see that this result is not so tragic. It could have been if you were more invested in the relationship, but you aren't. Why not look at it this way—you had a nice time together and became close friends. Now it's over. End of story."

"But if Chad hadn't died, Sam would have kept up the pretense that I was the one. How would you feel if that happened to you?"

"Perhaps you should ask Nate."

Scarlett gaped, and Violet shrugged.

"I knew it wasn't working, so I called time on our relationship. He wasn't happy about that. The person not doing the breaking up or breaking hearts can hardly complain if the other person takes exception."

"Seriously?" Scarlett wasn't sure how this had turned into a lecture, and she was the student. "You think that's the same? You and Nate never got further than a few kisses."

"And you did?"

"Well, no. But neither of you had anyone else waiting in the wings."

Violet's cheeks were suddenly pink, and she looked away.

Scarlett had hit a nerve. "Nate loves someone else?"

"It doesn't have to be all or nothing, you know. And no, it wasn't really Nate's problem."

"You?" Scarlett thumped down on the bed staring at her sister who'd suddenly turned into a stranger.

"You're so dramatic. I told you how I didn't feel about Nate the way I should. When I went to Portland to sell the family heirloom, I realized that I was happy doing my own thing. You know that I don't intend to be stuck in Cozy Hollow indefinitely."

This was another reminder that Violet felt trapped here. With all the drama, it had been pushed to the back of Scarlet's mind. Now her heart ached worse than ever, but she wouldn't let Violet see.

"So, then, it's nothing like Sam and me?" Scarlett blustered.

"Have it your way." Violet half-heartedly smoothed down the bed. "I was just trying to help."

"Yeah, great pep-talk. We need to get to work."

Feather's ruffled; they fed Bob and George and endured a silent trip to the café.

Dawn would arrive soon, but the sky looked heavy, and by the time they entered the town, a few large drops hit the van's windscreen. At the kitchen door, Violet found a note pinned down with a large stone, and they raced inside as the skies opened and rain thundered on the roof.

"That was lucky. Who's the note from?" Scarlett asked as she turned on the lights and shut the door.

Violet held the paper out to her. "I've no idea. There's no signature."

Scarlett read, *if you want to know what happened, come to Carver's Rest tonight. Alone.* She turned the paper over. The other side was blank.

Violet frowned. "That's part of the Turner's property."

"Mmmm. More correctly, it's the grounds of the factory and mill. Nighttime would be pretty scary with all those woods around."

"You can't seriously be thinking about going there?" Violet exclaimed.

"I don't want to," Scarlett admitted. "But what if it's our only chance to find out who killed Chad?"

"You just had your heart stomped on," Violet reminded her. "Is this a good time to be solving a crime?"

Scarlett shrugged. "As you so rightly pointed out, maybe my heart is still intact. Since I've never been in love, maybe I just bounce back quicker from disappointment."

"Wow, you're really going, aren't you?"

"I'm glad I can still impress you," Scarlett teased. While glad she could make light of her situation; she was nowhere near as inwardly calm as she pretended to be. Or, as accepting.

Violet flipped on the oven. "You'd impress me more by telling Nate."

"Actually, I thought I'd call him." Scarlett pulled out the flour. What would he think of the note and her intention? She could make a decent guess.

CHAPTER FIFTEEN

Nate arrived long before they were due to open the café. As usual, he came to the back door, armed with a wary look. Scarlett didn't bother with pleasantries, simply wiping her hands she ushered him inside.

"Here's the note, but before you say anything, it was under a stone at our back door with no envelope, and without knowing what it said, we both handled it," Violet informed him as she wrapped her arms around her middle.

Scarlett held the note by her forefinger and thumb as if this could rectify anything. "Obviously, we wouldn't have if we'd known it was evidence."

"Whoa." Nate reached out to her. "I get that you're upset, but if you'd stop waving it around and lay it on the table, I could actually read it," he instructed.

His logic was sound, and Scarlett did as he asked. Nate took out gloves from one of his handy and plentiful pockets and slipped them on. After reading the note, he turned it over. Only he elected to use a pair of tweezers pulled from yet another handy pocket and smoothed out the corners.

"Scarlett can't go alone," Violet stated.

Nate looked up in astonishment. "I wouldn't let her, and what makes you think the note was for Scarlett?"

That momentarily stopped Violet in her tracks. "Who else could it be meant for?"

"You both work here," he pointed out.

"Scarlett's the one with her nose in everybody's business," Violet reminded him.

She should be mad at her sister, but seeing these two continue with their needling made it hard to concentrate on what they should be discussing—such as, who sent the note?

"She may be the ringleader, but I seem to recall that you've had your fingers in as many of the pies." Nate placed the note in a plastic bag and sealed it.

"You may have noticed since you're so clever, that her pies are much deeper and richer than mine." Glaring at Nate, Violet tapped her foot furiously.

Out of the blue, laughter bubbled up and out of Scarlett. She laughed so hard that fat tears rolled down her cheeks, even as she apologized. "I'm so sorry. This is not funny at all, but oh, my, gosh. Your face, Vi. Your face!" she gasped.

Violet crossed her arms, tapping a foot even faster, waiting for Scarlett to control herself. "Please, excuse, my sister, Sheriff. She's become a little unhinged."

Scarlett snorted loudly, then wondered if she was in real danger of hysteria when it seemed to take forever to calm down. Nate's raised eyebrow and small smirk finally helped, and after several hiccups, Scarlett decided that she needed water and strong coffee.

"Are you okay to talk?" Nate inquired with a straight-face.

She took in a deep breath and held it for a moment before exhaling loudly. "I think so."

"Good. So what's all this about?" Nate held out the bag containing the note.

Taking a large gulp of water, Scarlett felt better. Laughing was supposed to be good medicine. "I'm guessing, but to me, it appears that someone has come to their senses and wants to help us solve the case."

"There could be other motives and Violet's right in saying that you can't go there alone."

Scarlett nodded. "But you do think someone has to go?"

Nate placed the bag into a pocket. "I'll decide who goes if I deem it necessary."

"If I don't go, maybe they won't bother to show themselves to a stranger or the law. It could be a wasted opportunity."

He frowned at her obvious wheedling. "The sheriff's department doesn't approve of using people as bait."

"What if it's Sam or Lexie who sent the note?" Violet asked casually.

Too casually for Scarlett, who glared at her sister. Violet looked away but not before Nate's interest was piqued.

"Do you have something you need to tell me? Either of you?"

"Sam and Lexie are in love," Violet blurted. "They have been for a long time."

For the first time since they'd known him, Nate's demeanor slipped. "That's not possible."

"It's not only possible but a fact," Scarlett assured him stoically.

Nate ran a hand through his hair. "Start at the beginning, because it's clear that this is just a tip of the iceberg and there's a heap more that I don't know. Again. Although, why I should be surprised by that is beyond me."

When Violet's explanation about Sam and Lexie drew to an embarrassing conclusion, Nate shook his head. "I'm sure I would have known if that's how Sam feels. Whenever we had a beer together, he spoke of you, not Lexie. You were the one he always talked about helping and welcomed the opportunity to brainstorm ideas and ways to make them happen. This makes no sense."

"Yet, it is Lexie he loves, not me." Scarlett, who'd decided that she should get back to work, began to load up cupcake trays with paper cups.

Nate watched her for several moments. "You're very calm about this."

"How am I supposed to react?" Scarlett removed the random papers, then replaced them in lines of the same color. "Nothing I say or do can change how Sam feels about Lexie or me, so I have to accept that we weren't meant to be. It's not like we were engaged or anything."

Slowly he nodded. "That's a good way to look at it, but it does highlight the fact that we both missed clues around the whole relationship. Which means they're good at hiding their feelings."

"If the only thing standing in their way were Chad, there would be your motive. The assumption that they planned his death is natural, but I know they didn't and that Chad's death wouldn't change a thing." Scarlett felt justified in her statement, regardless that it was weird to talk this way about Sam.

Nate came closer. "I haven't assumed anything, but how can you be so sure that they didn't plan this or another future together?"

Scarlett used an ice-cream scoop to fill the papers. "I found Chad alone. Lexie was in the tent the whole time, and she was the one who asked me to look for her husband."

"Sam wasn't in the tent," Nate reminded her. "And just because they weren't with each other doesn't mean they didn't plan it together."

"Lots of the bridal party disappeared around that time," she countered. "Besides, this is Sam we're talking about."

He nodded again. "Yes, and it's clear that none of us knew him as well as we thought."

Balling cookie dough Violet jumped in. "Harboring feelings for someone isn't a crime. Given the circumstances, I guess he was trying to move on with his life the best way he could."

Nate stiffened. "He didn't have to use Scarlett that way."

"Anyone he chose would be in the same situation," Violet noted.

While appreciating Violet's defense of Sam, despite being angry with him herself, Scarlett wasn't so happy with Nate's comments. She swiped at the mess of a forcefully placed dollop of batter and started that cupcake again.

"Whatever the situation was or is, I need more evidence," Nate said a little more evenly.

Scarlett put the trays in the oven. "Then I think you should look at the book in the library. The pictures are the same as in the Turner's house and will give you some idea as to how everyone fits in with the club. A club that, in my humble opinion, warrants a lot more investigation."

Nate ran his fingers through his hair. "I suppose I'd be wasting my breath asking you to step back from the investigation for the hundredth time, but I guess it won't hurt to look at this book. Especially because trying to get information from anywhere else is proving to be as hard as getting blood from a stone."

It was the first time Nate had admitted that the people who ran the Carver Corporation could be deliberately holding back information. It was obvious to Scarlett, and it was good to know that she wasn't imagining things.

Violet checked her watch. "Ruby will be at the library by now. Why don't you wait here and I'll run and get it. No sense in alerting the town about what we're looking at and feeding the gossip."

Nate glared and nodded simultaneously. Being bossed around by Violet still seemed to stick in his craw. Not bothered by his annoyance, Violet grabbed an umbrella and was out the door before he could change his mind.

Scarlett poured them both coffee, and he gave her a tight smile.

"You and your sisters are going to make me old before my time."

"That's not our intention," Scarlett said seriously. "The thing is, like it or not, my family's involved for so many reasons, and I can't ignore that. Also, don't think I'm not upset over this business with Sam. I simply don't want to look more of a fool than I am by letting everyone see it. Or having it trouble my sisters more than necessary."

Nate looked over his cup. "It's nobody's business."

"In Cozy Hollow?" She managed a small laugh. "There's no chance I'd be lucky enough for the town to let this slide." Scarlett finished off the cookies Violet had been balling, which gave her something to focus on. "In one respect, Lexie and Sam might be free to get together, but they certainly won't find it easy. The Turners will fight them to ensure she marries one of their own. Plus, the decision may involve the whole Carver Corporation, since they seem to have clear guidelines or patterns of how to live."

Nate came closer. "So, someone else will be encouraged to take Chad's place, but it can't be Sam?"

"That's what Lexie said, and she wasn't happy about it."

They stood staring at each other lost in their thoughts until Violet burst through the kitchen door, slightly breathless.

"I'd forgotten how heavy this thing is." She let the book thud onto the table and wiped her hands on her jeans.

Carefully, Scarlett opened it to the page with the original settlers. "This is where the Carver Corporation began."

"This doesn't prove any of the current families are related to these people," Nate pointed to the names under the grainy pictures. "They're all different from the ones that live at Harmony Beach.

"That's what we thought before Ruby showed me the American translations." Scarlett wiped her hands on a towel before reaching behind him to grab her laptop. Typing one of the names into a translation app, it turned into one that was all too familiar. "Aleksandr Tokar becomes Alexander Turner."

"Neat trick, but this guy lived several generations ago," Nate protested.

"Yes, but the family has a tradition of using the names over and over. Maybe not every generation, but the people in Harmony Beach are definitely related to these men."

"I'm sure another Chad won't appear anywhere," he mused.

"I admit it is an odd name when you compare it to the others, and I did wonder why he wasn't named after his father. Anyway, I'll show you the rest."

Pavel Okhotnik translated into Paul Wood. Iliya Dzhonson - Elijah Johnson. Piter Uitli became Peter Whitley.

Nate gave little away as he closed the book. "Can I take this? I'd like to study it a little more."

"Do you have a library card?" Violet asked.

A hand going to one of his many pockets, Nate frowned when he realized she was teasing.

Scarlett smiled. "I don't suppose Ruby will mind. Now, what about the note?"

He ran fingers through his hair again. "You will promise to do as I say or I go alone."

"I promise." Scarlett put her hand out, and Nate looked at her in exasperation before solemnly shaking it.

"I'll pick you up from your home, and we'll go together."

Scarlett's heart thumped as she saw him out the door. She was anxious, but not about dealing with Sam or going out to

Carver's Rest. Her thoughts had become scattered, and she wanted to believe that being involved in solving this case would help take her mind off everything else. Then she might be able to focus on how she was going to deal with those other issues.

CHAPTER SIXTEEN

Over the hill, the sea sparkled in a small amount of moonlight before clouds covered it. Leaving the main road to Harmony Beach, Nate turned onto a large entrance, which split into another six roads. The four smaller ones led to the houses of the families who ran Carver Corporation. One had a sign saying, *'Carver Community,'* and the last road was wide enough for two large trucks to pass. It led to their destination—Carver's Rest.

It was an odd name for a place where rest was not the focus. The factory and mill were usually a hive of activity and employed many people from the surrounding areas and most of Harmony Beach residents. Scarlett's father had been a logger and had died on the job five years ago.

Maybe this was why she shivered or at least was part of the reason. The night was usually extra dark in the country, but with the rain and a hidden moon, the slickness of the roads was the only shade that wasn't black. Even the trees blended into one menacing shadow.

After a mile or so, Nate dimmed his headlights, which meant they had to crawl along to see the edge of the road.

Scarlett turned toward the driver's seat. In shadow, only Nate's eyes were visible, and these darted to the left and right. As soon as she got into his car, the sheriff reminded her how to conduct herself when they arrived. They hadn't spoken since. Nate's body language made it abundantly clear that he wasn't happy to have her with him, and he was now so focused on getting them to their destination safely that she surmised it wasn't a good idea to break his concentration.

The map she'd printed off showed a vast parking lot just before the main gates, but the real-life scale took her by surprise. The lot was full of lines of two kinds of trucks. Having researched the business with Ruby's help, she could tell that most of the vehicles were used for transporting lumber, the main product of the Carter Corporation. On these, the claw-like sides ensured the trees remained stable in transit. The other trucks had closed in rigid bodies with electric tailgates at the back. These were for shipping beautifully crafted furniture and sculptings that the carvers made on site.

The work they did at the factory, coming into view through the open gates, had a growing following around the world—even at the unbelievable prices some of the top-end pieces sold for. Scarlett and most people she knew could only fantasize about owning anything that came out of this place.

Nate pulled his car up outside the vast factory covering a couple of acres and loomed over them.

Scarlett whispered, "It must be very old. Are we sneaking in?"

"Not exactly sneaking, but we don't want all the families to descend if they hear or see our car. At least, not right away and with no warrant. That would probably scare off the person who wants to meet with us."

She sucked in a breath. Being nervous about coming here was mainly centered around this being a ruse to get her out of the picture.

"Are you okay? You could stay in the car."

Scarlett licked her dry lips. There was no denying she was scared, but staying in the car wasn't an option. It was dark, and the person they were meeting was unknown. Still, Nate had an excellent track record of catching his man and knew how to use the gun he carried.

"I'm fine. Shall we take a look around and see if the author of that note is here?"

Thankfully, he didn't argue. "Do you have the map?"

Pulling it from her jacket pocket, she opened it over the console between them.

Nate shone a flashlight over the outline of the building, turning the paper so that it lined up with what they saw outside. "We'll walk along here," he pointed to the front of the building on the map. "If he's a no show, we'll still check the perimeter of the whole place. It could get wet out there, so do up your jacket." Folding the map, he put it in one of his breast pockets and opened the door.

Not wanting to be left behind, Scarlett scrambled out and hurried after him. He'd been right about the rain, which seemed to get heavier as soon as they got outside. By-passing the main entrance, they followed a line of massive roll-up doors.

A growl came from the end of the building, where large shrubs conveniently hid whatever made that sound.

Nate pushed her behind him. "Stay still."

She didn't need telling twice. The growl got louder, and eventually, a large pit-bull came into view. Then, a blinding light shone in their faces.

"You're trespassing," came a rough, slightly accented voice.

The man behind it was huge. She couldn't see his face and wasn't sure if she wanted to. Rain dripped from her chin and eyelashes, and she resisted the urge to wipe them, blinking rapidly instead. She was aware that Nate's hand already rested on his hip, where his firearm sat.

"I'm Sheriff Adams."

"Prove it."

The dog growled, and the man said something in another language. The animal obediently sat but continued his rumblings. Slowly, Nate reached into his jacket with his other hand, removed his badge from his shirt and held it out to the giant.

After peering at it closely, the man nodded, keeping his face in the dark. "What do you want here?"

Nate slipped his badge into a jacket pocket. "To have a look around Carver's Rest."

"Why?"

"There was a murder a few days ago." Nate's voice was even. In total contrast to Scarlett's somewhat erratic breathing.

"That is nothing to do with us."

"Us?" Nate was almost conversational. "Who does that encompass?"

"The people of Carver's Rest and the area beyond." The voice was proud and defiant.

Scarlett really wanted to know who he was. "Would you mind directing your flashlight elsewhere."

"I've seen you before," he said, giving her no indication if that was a good thing.

Scarlett peered across the space. It made no difference. "I'm sure I'd say the same if I could see your face."

The giant hesitated before pointing his flashlight to the ground. "You should come back when it's light. I'm sure Mr. Turner will be happy to show you around then."

"I'd like to look around while there's no activity. I know how busy it gets around here with trucks in and out. Since I'm here, perhaps you could show us around the place instead?" Nate suggested.

"I don't think so."

"If there's nothing to hide, then it should be fine. Otherwise, I can come back with a search warrant."

The giant hesitated. "I cannot take you inside."

"That's fine. We can do that part tomorrow."

"Come," he ordered.

Scarlett wasn't much shorter than Nate, and they both had to walk briskly to keep up with the man.

"What's your name?"

"Alex. I am the night security. You should know that the cameras are on us."

She couldn't help glancing around them to see if what he said was true, while Nate focused solely on Alex.

"I've seen them before. Your security is pretty impressive."

"Yes. It was costly and probably not so necessary now that I am here."

There didn't seem to be any gloating attached to his statement. Wearing a long trench coat, he looked very bulky, in a powerful way and capable of defending the factory from any trouble—along with the dog who followed the man closely.

Scarlett wondered if he was strong enough to turn a dinghy by himself and yet careful enough that he left no trace of having been on the beach. "You must be lonely out here by yourself," she ventured, marveling at how her hands were sweating while the rest of her body was cold.

"I have Boris."

Hearing his name, the dog licked a large hand.

"He's nice." Scarlett couldn't think of another adjective that wouldn't offend.

"No, he is not."

Scarlett couldn't see Alex's face but fancied she heard amusement in his voice.

"At least, he is not nice to others if they misbehave. With me, he is different."

"Dogs are clever," Scarlett agreed. "They know who's a threat and who can be trusted. My family just got a new dog."

He looked down at her. His eyes shone out of the dark as if they could pierce her thoughts. "I hear that you took in this dog that no one else wanted."

So, Alex knew who she was. He had to be the person behind the note, but would she scare him off if she brought it out into the open? She decided to be quiet and let Nate decide if things should take their natural course or not. "That's right. His name is Bob."

"And you have a cat."

This was not a question and made Scarlett wonder how or why he had information on her personal life. "Yes, his name's George. They're both very clever."

"Not as clever as Boris." Without preamble, Alex pointed at the doors. "Each one is big enough for tree trunks of any size."

Nate went closer and studied the doors for a moment before turning back to them. "Where do people park?"

"Around the back. It is dangerous here during the day."

Although he spoke casually, there lingered an unspoken menace behind the words, and Scarlett peered into the darkness around them. A large spotlight perched under the eaves on the corner of the building. If it were in use, it would light up this area like Christmas in Cozy Hollow.

Nate wiped the rain from his face. "The four roads leading to the owner's homes, do they go anywhere else?"

"No," Alex said emphatically.

"So anyone driving here can get to those houses but nowhere else."

"Yes."

Ignoring Boris, who emitted a long low growl, Nate stepped in front of Alex, having to tilt his head back to see the man's dark eyes. "Did you know Chad?"

Alex shrugged. "Everybody knows him. He was a good man, and I liked him."

Scarlett heard only sincerity, and Nate seemed satisfied.

"Can you think of anyone who might have a reason to harm him?"

Alex moved away. "I don't know about other people. You should leave soon, so I will quickly show you the other side of the building."

He walked briskly around the corner, forcing Nate and Scarlett to jog to keep up. This side had several high windows, and the rest of the wall was blank. Alex didn't stop until they'd rounded the next corner.

They were at the back of the building, where another, smaller parking lot branched out to the left. Creating in and out options, it curved back around past the heavily carved door which broke up the wall, along with many tall windows. As they walked, Scarlett noticed that the immediate line of parking spaces facing the building had a small sign in front of each close to the pavement.

"Is this the visitor's parking area?" Nate asked when they stood under the welcome shelter of an awning over the door.

"Yes." Alex pointed at the spaces with the signs. "The bosses park here."

Despite the rain, the security light above allowed them to see Alex and the area around them much better. His face was angular, but not unattractive, and his eyes were almost black. The dog didn't look any friendlier.

"And the workers," Scarlett wondered aloud, "where do they park?"

"They come on a bus from the Carver Community, which isn't far, but so many cars would take up too much space."

"I've seen it." Scarlett had driven through the pretty village once or twice. It seemed rather small to provide all the labor for this busy factory and the mill.

Nate echoed her thoughts. "Surely they don't all live there?"

"Most do. It is a friendly community, and there is a store." Alex said as if it was a wonderful place to live.

Nate frowned. "A village store wouldn't hold everything, so the residents would have to drive to Cozy Hollow or further for anything else they need, right?"

Alex stiffened. "The store has most things, and the manager is good at sourcing anything he does not stock. There is also a cinema, the beach, a playground, and a school. There is nothing more they require."

Sounding more and more like a commune, Scarlett kept this opinion to herself. "Do you live there?"

"I live here."

His voice was neutral, and Scarlett studied the building once more. It was extremely tall, but because of the windows' shape and size, Scarlett was sure it was only one level. "You live inside the factory?"

"There is a small house in the wood." Alex stared at her, an inscrutable look on his Slavic features. "It is better to be close to watch for arsonists, vandals, or thieves."

"Even with cameras all around the site?" she reminded him.

His eyes narrowed. "Cameras would be useless if there was a fire."

"Mmmm," she agreed. "A fire would be awful in a place like this."

Alex growled similarly to the way his dog had. "You have asked many questions. It is time for you to go."

When she would have mentioned the note, Nate put a firm hand on her arm, saying, "Thank you for your time, Alex."

The three of them walked back the same way. Boris sniffed at Scarlett's heels, but she didn't attempt to pat him. He was a working dog, and it would be foolish to treat him like Bob.

Alex waited in the rain while Nate turned the car around and was still there as they drove away.

Scarlett watched in her wing mirror until the rounded the first corner. "Well, that was enlightening, apart from not confirming if he was the one who left the note. Why didn't you want to ask?"

Nate tapped his hand on the wheel. "Alex had every opportunity to own up that he left the note, so either he didn't want to admit it in front of me or had nothing to do with it."

"I don't understand. Did you see the way he stared and how much he knew about me? It had to be him."

Nate raised an eyebrow, his gaze dedicated to the road. "He could have been looking at you because you're an attractive woman."

Scarlett emitted a small sound of surprise, and Nate coughed before continuing.

"If it was him, he'd made a point of you coming alone. He was never willingly going to impart any information with me by your side."

"But you're the law. If you ask him outright, he'd have to say if he knows anything."

Nate snorted. "There are plenty of citizens here and around the country who do not share your righteousness regarding my profession. I do wonder if he'll be in a hurry to tell his boss we were there. Although it's a moot point, as I'll have to front up to see Mr. Turner tomorrow and explain why we decided to look around his premises without asking him first."

"But why, if he doesn't know?" Scarlett shivered, and it wasn't purely from the rain dripping down her neck. Neither Mr. nor Mrs. Turner were pleasant to deal with, and she didn't envy Nate his task.

"As head of the corporation, Mr. Turner has eyes and ears everywhere, to say nothing of the security tapes. He'll eventually find out, and I'd rather not alienate the man altogether. I've already seen how he responds to questioning, and it wasn't pretty. If he thinks I'm sneaking around, he's going to circle the wagons more tightly, and we don't want that."

She did like the sound of that *we*, although it was undoubtedly a slip of the tongue. "Will you tell Mr. Turner that Alex or someone from here sent me a note?"

"Now, that's a different matter. Sometimes it's better to know something no one else does, and since we aren't certain it was the security guard, there's no point in having Mr. Turner conduct a witch hunt or get Alex in trouble. He could be a valuable ally."

Staring out the window at the landscape reminiscent of a horror movie, Scarlett decided that this made some sense. "But if you tell Mr. Turner about our visit and Alex didn't say anything, he'll be in trouble anyway."

Nate tapped on the wheel once more. "Hmmm."

"At least we got to see the place. I don't imagine that gate is often left open."

"It did seem odd," Nate agreed.

"As if we were expected, which we were. And that means no one else was on site to open the gate, right?"

"If the security system is as good as I imagine, Alex would have seen or been alerted somehow to us approaching."

"Would he have time to unlock the gates and get back to the factory or the woods behind it?"

Nate rubbed his chin. "He could have circled back behind us."

"That's true. But Alex could have chosen to keep the gates locked and not let us in."

"Maybe he thinks we'll be appeased by having a look around with relatively no fuss, and decide not to go back and recheck the place."

This was interesting, yet Nate didn't sound entirely convinced by his suggestion. "Who do *you* think *they are*?"

He shifted restlessly. "You won't stop until I admit that it has to be all four families involved somehow."

She was relatively successful in not grinning. "Not just Mr. Turner?"

"One man working alone isn't feasible in this scenario," he admitted. That theory doesn't take into account that this venture started with four men whose long history, and rules have dictated that this legacy must be abided by. The four in charge now, have made it clear that they have no intention of changing. I looked into the whole set-up, and I agree that the Carver Corporation is living in the past to a great extent, but it's a business supplying jobs to the community and taking care of it in many other ways. It operates to the edge of the law, yet has never crossed over as far as I know."

This space, where they discussed a case as if her opinion mattered, meant a great deal to Scarlett. "You mean that murder, especially of one of their own, feels like a step too far?"

"It's not something I can prove or disprove yet. . ."

"Stop!" Scarlett yelled, her hand shooting out to the dash-board as the car lurched and shuddered.

"What the heck?" Nate roared. "I could have killed us!"

Leaning forward, she pointed to the tree closest to her. "Look at how there are no branches at a certain height. I bet there are cameras along here."

Nate groaned and adjusted his seat belt, which was probably digging into his chest the way hers was.

"Thanks for pointing that out and nearly giving me a heart attack."

"Sorry. I wanted to make sure that my eyes weren't playing tricks." She pointed. "Now that we're right beside it, I can see a metal box up there."

"It's best if we don't hang around on this road." Nate slipped the car out of neutral. "I'll come back tomorrow and check out your theory about the gate and cameras."

Satisfied, Scarlett leaned back in her seat. "So, bringing me along wasn't the worst idea?"

"We both know you would have come out here with or without me. But I don't want you to be under the illusion that I won't lock you up if you decide to take on this case yourself."

His terse words reminded Scarlett that he'd felt like he had no choice, and instead of lightening the mood which had been her intention, she'd made him once more resentful.

They drove home in the same way they'd arrived— solemn and lost in their thoughts.

CHAPTER SEVENTEEN

*W*e need to talk.

No one likes to wake up to that kind of text. The moment she turned on her phone and saw it, Scarlett felt her temper rise. It had been sent last night, along with many more. It was easy to ignore them when she was out with Nate embroiled on the mystery and slightly harder when she'd arrived home and faced her sisters' de-brief.

Not usually vindictive, Scarlett decided as she dressed that Sam could wait to have the conversation he so desperately wanted. After all, she'd had to wait to find out that her boyfriend was in love with another woman.

By the time she made her way to the kitchen, she'd gone through a dozen scenarios of what she would heatedly say to the paramedic lothario, and then her mood somersaulted into a frozen lake.

Sam sat at the kitchen table with a wary Ruby and a fuming Violet was making coffee. He was fortunate that this sister held no weapon. He jumped up as she entered.

"I wasn't expecting you," Scarlett managed stiffly, ignoring his awkwardness.

"I'm sorry to turn up unannounced, but you must know that I've tried to reach you a dozen times." He slid his hands into the pockets of his pants. "I have to get this off my chest, and I knew you'd avoid me if I asked for a meeting."

"And, again, this is all about you." Violet's sarcasm was well-founded.

Sam shook his head violently, keeping his eyes on Scarlett. "You don't understand. No one could have seen the change in circumstances."

"Seriously?" Violet glared. "That's your idea of an apology?"

Sam's cheeks reddened, but he wasn't backing down. Not a wise move, if he had any idea of how Violet's temper was akin to a caged beast when her sisters were upset.

"I have apologized. I do apologize, but this is more than that. Scarlett, I never considered what would happen if Lexie didn't marry Chad. The three of us were so close that I knew nothing I could say would change their minds, and despite how they felt, they'd go through with the wedding. I learned a long time ago to curb my feelings for Lexie, and that allowed us all to remain friends."

"Good for you!" Violet raged. "You get exactly what you want, but that's not so comforting for Scarlett."

"Can you let me finish? Please," Sam begged.

Violet sniffed disdainfully. "I don't know why you think you should be allowed to. Especially after practically forcing your way inside this house."

"Actually," Scarlett intervened. "I'd like to hear what Sam has to say. Then we can be done with the whole thing." She sat at the far end of the table and clasped her hands in her lap, steeling herself to hear why she wasn't good enough.

Sam hesitated before reclaiming his seat. Lifting his chin and looking her in the eyes was at least something. "After you found Chad, I felt this huge loss. His friendship meant the world to me, and Lexie was the only one who could possibly understand. I went to her for consolation and to tell her that it wasn't her fault."

"You never gave me the opportunity to try to understand, and the explanation is far too late," Scarlett retorted. "I was there, remember, trying to give you space. Trusting that's all you needed." Her anger flared and then was suddenly gone, replaced by loss and deep disappointment. Maybe he was still nice, kind, and caring, but Sam was also a coward.

Ruby hunkered in her chair, while unfortunately for him, Violet was still furious.

"So, we're supposed to believe that you didn't kill Chad so you could finally get Lexie?"

His head snapped around to her. "What? How can you ask me that?"

"Because we thought we knew you." Violet pulled a disgusted face. "We were mistaken about that, which makes me wonder what else we got wrong?"

"I made a mistake, maybe several," he protested. "As I said, there was no other scenario where I could manufacture this outcome. I've done all I could not to hurt Chad."

Ruby broke her silence. "Hurting Scarlett shouldn't have been an option either."

Sam hung his head. "You're right. I'll never be able to apologize enough, but I swear I did not kill Chad and never meant to hurt Scarlett."

Scarlett shouldn't feel sorry for him, but he looked so beaten. "Do you think Rebecca could have done it? Wasn't she in the same position as you, since she loved, Chad?"

He looked up, hopefully. "I haven't been thinking clearly since it happened, so I didn't give that any thought, but, yes, Rebecca could be guilty. I should talk to Nate. It might help get his department to back off Lexie and me."

"Oh, Sam." Ruby shook her head sorrowfully. "There are

more people to worry about than you and Lexie. Chad has a family, and others are suffering in other ways with all the doubts and suspicion."

Sam blanched at the softly spoken reprimand. "It's not like I haven't spent time with Chad's brother, but all the other men have been locked up together discussing Lexie's fate, and the women have been consoling Mrs. Wood, pretty much since it happened. Rebecca was never going to marry Chad. She loved him, but she understood that the older generation wouldn't allow it, just as I did."

"This is all so sick." Violet glared at Sam. "You can't force people to love each other."

"I feel the same way. Only, I had plenty of years to come to terms with it, and being Chad's friend meant accepting the strangeness. At least that's the way I justified it to myself."

Scarlett frowned, then fetched a notebook and a pen from the counter. "Could you please write down the hierarchy of the families?"

Relief washed over his features. "Of course." He barely thought about it before scribbling down a list.

Scarlett watched over his shoulder. The writing was different as she suspected it would be. Sam could be doing it differently on purpose, but she hadn't given him time to work on that when she'd fleetingly considered that he'd sent her the note. He worked fast and methodically, and soon there was a list of the last three generations.

"You said that Lexie would have to marry someone on this list, right?"

Sam tapped the pen on one name, then another. "In my opinion, Chad's brother, Michael, is the top option. Followed by the chief carvers son, David."

"Eww!" Violet gagged. "This is horrible."

"Yes, the timing is ugly, but apart from the lack of love, no one is related unless distantly in Russia," Ruby pointed out.

"If the Turners had a son, then a suitable bride would have been found from their hometown."

"What are Lexie's thoughts on this?" Scarlett was proud that she could discuss this reasonably and glad that the urge to yell at him had gone.

"She doesn't like any of them enough to marry," Sam said quietly.

Scarlett's heart sank. "But they'll force her to, and she still has no choice who it will be?"

"None. Her family will disown her if she doesn't comply with the board's wishes."

The idea of being handed around to the next best prospect was revolting and a terrible situation for Lexie. How long would they wait to announce another engagement, Scarlett wondered. Months? Weeks?

"Then she's complicit," Violet stated matter-of-factly.

"That's harsh, Vi," Ruby interjected. "We don't come from that world, so we don't know how it would feel."

Violet sniffed. "I know that no one will ever get to choose my husband, and the last time I checked in this day and age, a woman has rights."

Scarlett thought of Lexie and the lost look on her face. Having to marry without love for a second time, no matter that she might be allowed a few months to grieve, was heartbreaking. There was one option that no one had mentioned. "Why don't you elope?"

All eyes were on her as she spoke to Sam. "Unless money and power are all Lexie cares about, it makes perfect sense. Wouldn't you agree?"

"I don't have anything to offer her," Sam protested.

"You have a good job, and she could work. I know she wants to. This is no time to be a wimp." Scarlett shrugged. "If you want her so badly, then you have to make her believe you'll make it happen no matter the consequences."

"Scarlett!" Violet yelled. "This is beyond niceness. You don't have to make their lives easy."

Scarlett managed a small smile. "Mom would expect us not to make things harder for anyone just because we can."

"That's very noble, but have you given a thought to the fact that Lexie is recently widowed. There's no way she'll be contemplating marriage any time soon. It's simply not decent."

Sam nodded. "Violet's right—and wrong. Lexie loves me, and she's grieving, as am I. That doesn't mean another wedding won't be in the planning very soon."

"Since you seem to have an answer to any suggestion, you better tell us what you want from us?" Scarlett asked.

Sam's eyes glistened. "Definitely, your forgiveness, then help in finding the killer. I'm anxious they'll try again if a groom is announced or our secret is discovered. Nothing can go under the radar for long at that place, and it could be Lexie next time."

He didn't attempt to hide how scared he was, and it showed how much Sam loved Lexie that he would try anything to prevent her from being hurt—even asking his ex-girlfriend to help.

Scarlett took in a deep breath. "Even after all you've said, it was still wrong to let me believe that you were in love with me."

"I didn't lie, because I do love you—just not in the way I should," he finished lamely.

Scarlett sighed, weary of the conversation. "Is that supposed to appease me in some way? By not telling *all* the truth, you are as guilty as if you lied."

"You're right." Sam hung his head once more. "I can't justify it. I'm sorry, Scarlett. You don't deserve all this."

"That's a start. Anyway, you might have to wait for complete forgiveness, but the truth is I've been focusing on little else other than finding the murderer." Preferring to keep it quiet as Nate suggested, Scarlett omitted to tell Sam about the late-night drive. She stood and stretched, feeling a little lighter. "Now, we need to get to the café. We're already late."

Reluctantly he went to the door, hesitating before he opened it. "If you don't mind, I do have one suggestion." When she didn't object, he continued. "Lexie, overheard her mom say that the Carver community is bursting with speculation, but they've effectively closed ranks. Nate's been there, but they don't trust him, and the time I've spent with Lexie has made them watchful of me. If you went there, they might recognize you as the caterer, but it might be a better chance to get some information."

While it occurred to Scarlet that Sam wasn't too bothered by any danger, she might incur, she merely nodded. "I'll go there when I can." What that meant was defying Nate again, and she wasn't eager to do that so soon. However, waiting hadn't worked so far.

"Thank you, and thanks for listening. I am truly sorry, and I appreciate how unfair it is to ask a favor when you'd be perfectly within your rights to kick me off the property and never want to see me again."

Violet shut the door behind him with a bang, a certain gleam in her eyes. "He shouldn't tempt me. I can see that we aren't going to talk you out of this, so we'll all go. I'll make us a picnic this afternoon, and we'll have supper at the beach, so we have an excuse to look around."

Scarlett looked through the window, noticing for the first time that the rain had cleared and the sky was changing color. "Today? Are you sure? I don't know how safe it will be or what we'll find."

"Let's not give anyone time to figure out our plans. It's not a closed community, despite it having that feel about it.

We'll chat with people like we usually do and search for sea glass," Violet assured her.

"Okay. But we need to get a move on—we're so late." Scarlett pulled out a bag and began throwing in some herbs and tomatoes from the fridge.

Ruby pushed the chairs in. "Since I'm awake, I'll come and give you a hand to make up time."

"That would be fantastic. We may as well all go in the van. Be ready in 10 minutes." Scarlett ran down the hall to her room to get her bag thinking ahead to this afternoon. Nate surely wouldn't be upset over a picnic, right?

CHAPTER EIGHTEEN

With Ruby's help, and Violet taking time to chat with the customers relieving Scarlett from that duty, the day went without a hitch—until Olivia stopped by as they were closing.

"I'm glad I caught you before you left." Her usual smile was missing.

"Is something wrong?" Scarlett asked.

"I saw Ruby at lunchtime, and she told me about your trip to the Carver community this afternoon."

Scarlett sighed. She should have recalled that her sister could never keep a secret from Olivia. "We're curious and want to see first-hand how village life works. It has to be different from even our small town."

A delicate eyebrow arched. "Is that all there is to it?"

Keeping any guilt off her face was tricky for Scarlett, who didn't want to upset her aunt but didn't want her to come. "We're taking Bob for a run at the beach. We haven't done anything together for a while, and thought a picnic would be nice."

"That's hardly a quick trip," Olivia observed her. "Have you forgotten that there's a murderer on the loose?"

"Not at all, but it will be daylight, and there'll be people around." Scarlett cleaned off a table and carried a tray out to the kitchen.

Olivia followed like a mother hen. "Most of them are lovely from out that way, but we can be reasonably certain that one of them is not."

"As far as we know, no one's said that it's likely to be one of the villagers," Violet chipped in as she loaded up the basket.

"I don't exactly think it's someone from there, but other people visit it. Some from nearby," Olivia added pointedly.

Scarlett read through the thinly veiled subtlety. "So you've decided on the murderer being a family member?"

"Absolutely." Olivia nodded. "The only thing I'm not sure of is which family."

"But definitely one of the four?" Scarlett was secretly pleased to see Olivia just as invested in solving the crime as she was. It would make life easier.

"It has to be, and I can tell that you feel the same way."

Olivia was a little smug, but Scarlett couldn't lie. They'd had a couple of conversations about this very thing, and it made so much sense that the killer was someone Chad knew well. Someone who could get to the beach and away from it without arousing suspicion.

"I do, and it's so frustrating not to be able to chat with any of them, which is why we're heading out there now. Someone must have something to say that will be of value and point us in the right direction. Although, every lead we've had has been a dead end." She smiled wryly. "Just to reassure you, we'll be together, so there's no need to worry."

"Hah! As if I could ever stop worrying about the three of

you." Olivia sniffed. "You're all the family I have, and I don't want you getting in over your heads with this."

Scarlett wiped her hands so that she could hug her aunt. "I promise we'll be careful."

"Mind you do." Olivia sniffed again. "You should also know that George has been wandering the town, and he tried to attack a massive Pitbull today not far from here."

"Oh, no! Is George okay?"

"He wasn't harmed at all. In fact, the man, who I assumed was the dog's owner, pried George off after several scratches for his trouble and sent your cat on his way with no more than a stern talking to. The dog looked like he could bite George in half with his huge teeth, and wanted to, but he didn't move. It was as if he was waiting for the man's permission to retaliate."

Scarlett flinched at the scenario. "A pit-bull? The owner wasn't a giant, was he?"

Olivia laughed. "Now that you mention it, he was rather large. And very stern. Although I could see that he loves animals so he must be far nicer than he appears."

"It must be Alex." Scarlett murmured, wanting to kick herself.

Violet crossed her arms. "You know him?"

"I've met him once. He was the man I met at Carver's Rest," she admitted.

"What?" Olivia wasn't impressed. "You surely didn't go there? It's a dangerous place."

She'd deliberately not said anything to Olivia, to avoid lying about how scary the experience had been and also that it held the memory of being the place her father worked. "I was with Nate. We were supposed to meet someone, but it never eventuated."

"I guess that's better than taking your sisters," Olivia

grudgingly conceded. "Since you have plans, I'll see you tomorrow, and I expect a full account of this *picnic*."

"You dodged a bullet there," Violet smirked as soon as Olivia was out of ear-shot.

Scarlett locked the door. "A little help would have been great."

"I'm not lying to our Aunt." Violet helped load the last of the plates into the dishwasher.

"Really?" Scarlett shook her head. "Your conscience and memory are a little fickle these days."

"I don't know what you mean. Let's go and pick up the others."

Violet conveniently forgot how she'd changed her mind about pursuing a relationship with the sheriff and had taken ages to admit it, even to her sisters. Secrets had stacked up in this family for years, and only recently had they begun to fall like a giant game of Jenga.

Still, she had her own issues with Sam, and right now, she was more intent on solving Chad's murder than figuring out why she and her sisters couldn't find a man to be happy with. That was a mystery for another time and better headspace.

Collecting Ruby and Bob from the library—George was still AWOL—they headed out of town.

CHAPTER NINETEEN

Harmony Beach was well known for the expansive stretch of pristine white sand and, apart from the Turners *private* section, it was open to the public.

As they came down the last hill, a good deal of the beach came into view, along with the sparkling water stretching out to the empty horizon. It was a much better time of day and better weather in which to appreciate it.

Ruby pointed ahead through the van window. "I looked the title up, and no one owns any of the beaches along this part of the coast."

Scarlett nodded, having done the same thing. "You read my mind. I figured the Carver families spread the word it was private a generation or two ago, and now everyone takes it for granted that it must be so."

"That's just wrong," Violet stated. "No one person or family should own a beach."

"Does it matter when there's so much beach here anyway?" Ruby reasoned.

Violet snorted. "If everyone who lived by a beach decided that was the case, there'd be none left for the rest of us."

Scarlett agreed with Violet but didn't want to start an argument. She'd just realized that what she'd said to her aunt about the sisters not doing much together, except for work, was true. And just because they were on a mission this afternoon, didn't mean they couldn't enjoy the picnic.

The main road followed the beach and went through the middle of the Carver Community. A wall of stones was split in the middle by a large entrance and flower beds on either side were well-tended. Scarlett drove slowly, mindful of children, but interested in the configuration of the village.

"The houses are all the same," Violet noted.

"I guess it's cheaper to build so many that way," Ruby suggested. "A builder could buy things like windows and doors in bulk as well as fittings."

The road led to a reasonably sized store then curved back on itself. To the right of this was an area with a playground, including a soccer pitch. Several children stopped a game to watch them as they went by. Scarlett continued the circuit until they got to an impressive cedar with a beautifully carved seat underneath.

"This mini town is so cute," Ruby gushed. With the school by the park and the houses close by, it feels safe."

"Town of any description is a bit generous. " Violet peered around her. "It's more of a village in size."

"Those kids look really happy, so it must be a nice place to live."

Scarlett smiled at Ruby in the rear mirror. With the beach on one side and forest on the other, the place was a small haven. The van windows were down, allowing the warm air, sweet with the scent of flowers, yet salty from the sea to flow around them. Soft sounds of the surf and children's voices, plus the chatter of seabirds in the trees, made Scarlett and her sisters smile. Despite its limitations, the attraction of living in this idyllic place was completely understandable.

"Where shall we eat?" Violet leaned forward against her seatbelt.

Instead of enjoying the ambiance or focusing on why they were really here, Violet was already thinking of her stomach. Bob took the opportunity to thrust his head out of her window from behind, making Scarlett grin at his lolling tongue and delighted expression.

"There's a walkway to the beach," Ruby pointed between two houses.

Scarlett parked, and the three of them shared the load of the picnic basket, rug, and a flask of coffee. Bob ran up the beaten sandy path, which ended right on the beach. To the immediate left, there was a small grass area. "Let's drop everything there and take a quick look around before we eat."

Ruby was happy to, Violet, not so much, but she followed anyway. Further along the beach were a ramp, a dinghy, and two kayaks. Beyond them, a large stone wall separated this part of the beach from the Turners and was mirrored on the other side to close it off from the rest of Harmony Beach. Bob bounded along beside them, then darted down to the water, barking as it chased him back to the drier sand.

"He doesn't look like he's ever seen a beach," Ruby said sadly.

"Then he'll enjoy the trip even more," Violet consoled her.

"Those two walls make this a semi-private beach as well. Although, I guess people could come down the ramp." Scarlett mused.

"It is pretty secluded." Ruby agreed. "I didn't know it was here, did you, Scarlett?"

"I didn't before I looked it up on the map."

"With the Turners' snobbery, there's no way any of the people from here got an invite to the wedding. If they had, we might have heard people talking about the place."

Violet's scorn struck a chord with Scarlett. Alex spoke of the village as though he were proud of it, which meant he must have been here. Yet, no other member of the family or Sam had mentioned it. Not even Lexie, who lived so close, she must have been here. Was that deliberate? And if so, in what respect? To keep it safe or to hide it from the world. Both would have seemed silly a week ago, but the reality was, Chad was dead, and they had no real leads on who could have done it.

They walked back to the grass where Scarlett helped Violet with the rug. Ruby pulled out chicken, salad, and cupcakes to follow. They ate, looking out to the sea, enjoying the peace and food, lost in their thoughts. There was something about the sea air that increased appetite, and they made a significant dent in the picnic with Bob's help.

The dog had gone back to the water, running at it again and again. "He'll sleep well tonight," Scarlett laughed, handing out napkins. "Good job on the food, Vi. I'm looking forward to the cupcakes." About to pour coffee, she noticed a group approaching from the path. "Look, we have visitors."

Appearing to be the same ones from the soccer field, they inched forward as if fascinated and, at the same time, nervous of the strangers on their beach.

"Hello," Ruby called to them.

A girl of about ten came a little closer than the others. "What are you doing here?"

Ruby pointed at the basket and the remains of their food. "We're having a picnic."

The girl glanced at her companions, who simply stared. Giving an impatient shake of her head, she asked with more surety. "Why are you having it on our beach?"

Scarlett smiled. "This is our supper, and we came this way for a change of scenery. Your beach looked a nice place to eat."

"We don't eat at the beach," a younger boy by a year or so stated, half-hiding behind the girl.

"My sisters and I don't live near a beach," Ruby explained. "So coming here is a nice change for us."

The girl came closer still, dragging the boy along with her. "I haven't seen you here before, but I have seen you somewhere." Her eyes narrowed at Scarlett. "What's your name?"

"I'm Scarlett, and my sisters are Violet and Ruby."

The girl screwed up her button nose. "Aren't they colors?"

Scarlett grinned. "They are, but they can be names too. Our mom's name was Lilac."

"That's strange. I'm Althea, and this is Joe." She acknowledged the boy half a head shorter who couldn't possibly get any closer to the girl and remained half-hidden behind her.

"That's a pretty name," Ruby said.

"Thank you. It was my gran's. Where do you live?"

"In Cozy Hollow. Do you know it?" Scarlett spoke casually, wanting to know where the girl had seen her, but not wanting to frighten her off. Having only been out to the Turners three times in as many weeks, there'd been no time to look any further than the private beach. Had the girl seen her looking over the grounds? Of course, Scarlett had been out to Carver's Rest, but that was late at night, and it would have been a long wet trek for a child from the village.

The girl grinned delightedly. "We've all been to Cozy Hollow."

"Did you like it?" Scarlett asked.

"Oh, yes! We had ice cream at the diner."

Scarlett winced. The diner burnt down some time back and hadn't yet been rebuilt. "I love ice cream too."

Just then, Bob launched himself at the children, tail wagging and emitting soft woofs in delight at finding people more his size.

The children cowered behind Althea, which only encouraged Bob to join in his idea of hide and seek. He jumped at Joe and knocked him to the sand.

"Bob! Come here this minute!" Scarlett shouted.

Head down and tail between his legs; he slunk over to the rug. None of them had ever raised their voice to him, and he cowed on his belly as if he expected more than a growling.

It was upsetting for the family, and Scarlett pulled him onto her lap. It's okay, but you can't go scaring the children," she told him before explaining to the children, "He won't hurt you. Bob just wanted to play. Come and pat him."

It took a few minutes to reassure them, and then they were all over Bob like a rash. Bob rolled onto his back, and Scarlett could swear he smiled in delight as they fussed over him.

"How many people live here?" she asked casually.

"I don't know exactly." The girl shrugged. "But there are 20 houses. I counted them."

"And a store," Joe added importantly.

"And a school. My mom's the teacher." Althea's mouth turned down at the corners. "I'm probably going to be one too, but I'd rather be a driver."

It seemed that her candid manner was what put the girl in charge as the spokesperson, and Scarlett could tell by the tilt of head and tone that she was very proud to be in this position, despite her disappointment at not able to pursue a career she'd prefer. "Teachers and drivers are both cool. Are there other children, or is it just your group?"

"There are some babies," the boy ventured, before hiding again.

"What about big kids—teenagers?" Scarlett pressed.

"They work at the factory. There's a bus that takes them there and brings them home."

Scarlett had another question that seemed relevant. "Do you know Alex? He lives at the factory."

"We can't go the factory," Althea said firmly. "It's too dangerous."

Althea was studying her sisters, and even though the girl had expertly avoided answering the question about Alex, Scarlett continued in the previous vein. "Do all the other parents work there?"

The girl laughed. "Only dads get to work there. Except for the receptionist, all the moms stay here and look after the children, or tend the gardens."

"My mom works in the shop when I'm at school," Joe proudly told them.

It was like stepping back in time, and Scarlett had to keep a watch on Violet, whose annoyance meter was gaining traction. As much as she didn't appreciate the sentiment, the child before her was brought up to think this way, and Scarlett wouldn't contradict her beliefs.

"Are any of the men from here carvers?"

The little girl rolled her eyes, and the other children giggled. "Only people from the big houses do that."

With a certain amount of awe, they all looked in the direction of those four houses. Little was visible apart from the tips of roofs peeking out between trees.

Althea puffed out her skinny chest. "Most of our dads cut the logs and mill them or drive the trucks."

Joe crept around his friend. "My dad drives the biggest truck."

"They go right up the mountains and bring the logs down to the factory. Some are milled for buildings, and the carvers use the rest. My dad takes the carvings to the people who buy them. Sometimes he drives for days. It's very important, and he has to drive very carefully," Althea said pointedly, giving Joe a side-eye.

"I'm sure he does. I've seen some of the carvings at the Turners' house," Scarlett admitted. "They are all beautiful."

Several little mouths gaped open.

"You've been inside?" Blinking rapidly, Althea put her hands to her cheeks, much like the home alone kid.

"We all have." Violet explained, waiting a moment while the girl dealt with her amazement, before adding, "We made some food and the cake for the wedding."

"The wedding? You mean when the man died?" Althea informed them as casually as if she was reciting a nursery rhyme.

CHAPTER TWENTY

S hocked, Scarlett shook her head at Violet, who was about to launch into goodness knew what kind of questioning. Now that they were getting somewhere, Scarlett was warier than ever of scaring them off. "You heard about that?"

"I saw him. He was yelling at another man, but I didn't hear exactly what he said," Althea said with disappointment.

Scarlett sucked in a large breath. Ruby and Violet had their hands clasped in their laps, their knuckles whitening. "Can you show me where you saw them arguing?"

The children fidgeted, looking about them as if they expected someone to come out of the long grasses to the right of them or down the path.

"There's a shortcut," Althea admitted cagily before eyeing up the basket. "Do you have any sweets?"

"No sweets, but we do have cupcakes." Ruby pulled out a container and held it open to the group."

Joe ran his tongue ran around his lips. "You made these?"

"My sister did," Ruby nodded towards Violet.

Althea's hand twitched, but she looked up at the sun. "It

will be time to go home soon, so we need to hurry. We'll have them when we get back."

The group turned, but Althea ran to head them off. "You can't come with Joe and me. There's too many of you. Go home, and we'll play tomorrow." Althea shooed the younger ones, but they stopped several feet away, eyeing the container, along with Bob.

"Fine." Althea sounded like a much older person exasperated by her charges. "Take the cupcakes, but eat them before you go home, or we'll all be in big trouble, and you better save some for Joe and me."

Happy with their bribe, the children eagerly took one each from Ruby and tore off the wrappers with glee. Ruby frowned and raced around collecting the paper, so it didn't blow around the beach or end up in the sea. When she got back, Violet and Scarlett had packed up their picnic leftovers.

The children sat in a circle, frosting smearing their faces. Bob couldn't get any closer to them and delicately accepted small morsels.

Ruby winked at her sisters. "I better stay with them to make sure the little ones don't go into the water, and Bob might be more of a hindrance if he goes with you."

Scarlett nodded gratefully. "Good idea." She lowered her voice. "Plus, we'll know where they are and won't be following us. We'll leave the picnic stuff here and pick it up on the way back."

Then she and Violet followed Joe and the impatient Althea back to the main street. The next cul-de-sac held another access at the end, and since their guides practically ran the whole way, they had to walk faster to keep them in sight.

"Why couldn't we just walk along the rocks to Turners' section of the beach?" Violet huffed.

"Didn't you notice the fence? The only way we'd get

around that would be to swim, and the water isn't warm enough for me."

Violet nodded. "I saw it, and I'm sure we could have climbed it. Besides, it seems silly to have a fence with all these walkways."

"Perhaps it's used as a deterrent. If the kids come here by themselves, they could get hurt on the sharp rocks."

Violet huffed once more. "I guess that could be the reason."

They came out of the walkway onto the far end of the Turners' beach. With the rocks at their back, Scarlett wondered if the separation was man-made to keep the workers away from the four families or to keep the community free of visitors.

The children called them from almost halfway along, and the sisters picked up their pace, although it was hard going in the soft sand.

Scarlett plucked at Violet's shirt. "Let's go back up to the grass line where the sand's firmer."

It was indeed easier, and soon they were beside the children. Hands on hips, Althea pointed in front of her. "This is where the men were fighting."

One noticeable thing about the vista was that the beach was empty. No boat. It did look about right to Scarlett, and she'd confirm with Violet later. If Althea were telling the truth about witnessing the fight and possibly more, the case would be solved. It was exciting, and she had difficulty keeping her voice even.

"Apart from the men, do you remember what was here that day?"

"Mr. Turner's dinghy was the only thing on the beach. Althea pursed her lips. It was kind of strange because he only uses it to get to his big boat, and we never saw that, did we, Joe?"

The boy shook his head but remained silent. It must have been a scary thing for children to see, and Scarlett smiled encouragingly at him.

Violet nodded at the glistening water. "I wonder where the boats are."

"The big boat is always at the marina on Harmony Beach —the main part—unless the family is going to use it," Althea spoke knowledgeably.

"And do you know where the dinghy would be now?"

The girl nodded. "After the police left, we watched them drag it down to the water, and then they pulled it along to the little jetty near the big house where it gets tied up. You know, no one has to row it, though. An engine gets put on the back," she explained.

Scarlett walked further into the grass line. It had a slight incline, and when she stood at the top, she could see a little more of the four houses. "How do the people from the other three houses get down to this beach?"

Althea pointed a few feet to Scarlett's right. "There's a path. You can't see it because of the long grass, but it's there."

The five of them walked to the place Althea had indicated, and sure enough, when Scarlett pulled back the grass, a wide groove became visible. The path would only permit single file.

The children watched everything she did, and Scarlett appreciated that they were curious, which helped with choosing the questions she could ask. "Did you hear what the men said?"

"Not really," Althea admitted. "But they were both very angry."

Scarlett made a mental note. "Did they come from the Turners' place?"

"Only one of them. The short man came from this path.

The man on the beach walked quickly to the boat and went to the short man when he arrived."

"Do you know who they were?"

Althea looked to a wide-eyed Joe who chewed his lip. "The tall man was the groom. We saw him getting married to the blonde lady. He walks on the beach with her sometimes."

Scarlett swallowed hard because that would never happen again. Luckily Violet took over for a moment.

"How did the boat look? Was it up on its side or flipped over?"

Althea pursed her lips again as she thought about this. Then her eyes lit up. "The boat was on its side."

"The dinghy wasn't small. How did it stay on its side?" Violet mused.

"A piece of wood was wedged underneath," Joe shyly offered.

Scarlett smiled her thanks. "Where were you two when they were fighting?"

"In the grass. We aren't supposed to come here, and we'd get in trouble if our parents found out we did. We just wanted to watch the wedding. It was very fancy," Althea sighed.

Who says a driver can't love a pretty dress and a moving ceremony? Scarlett mused before taking note of Turner's property from this angle. She could see a good deal of the backyard and where the wedding tent would have been, but the children were significantly shorter than her. "Could you see any of it from here?"

"Not really. We saw the tops of their heads under the arch. But when they went to the jetty to have their photos taken, we could see them better because it slopes down to the steps and the ramp."

Scarlett knew this to be accurate, which made it easier to believe Althea about the rest. "The groom came to the boat by himself, and apart from the short man, was anyone else here?"

"No, just them," the girl said." It was hard for the man to flip the boat by himself."

Scarlett hesitated to ask another question that burned to get out. It was one thing to talk about where people were, but asking the children about the murder was awkward. What if she upset them?

Violet had no such compunction. "How did the small man kill the tall man?"

Althea wasn't fazed at all. In fact, she demonstrated on Joe.

"They yelled for a bit, then tall man headed back to the party, but he didn't get more than a couple of steps. The small man ran after him with an oar and hit the tall man on the back of the head."

"Oww." Joe clutched his head where she had whacked him and moved quickly out of reach.

Althea gave him a dismissive glance. "It wasn't that hard. Don't be a baby."

Scarlett intervened. "What happened next?"

"The man was on his face, and the short man pushed him over onto his back then pulled the boat over on him."

Scarlett's insides churned. If Althea could identify the killer, the case would be closed—yet it seemed too easy. "You're very clever to have noticed and remembered all this, Althea. Why didn't you tell the sheriff or a deputy when they came?"

Althea dug her toes in the sand and looked up from under her bangs. "I told you, we're not supposed to come near here or talk to outsiders."

Joe continued to rub his head as he looked warily around them. "We'll be in big trouble if my dad finds out."

"My mom's scarier than our dads." Althea grimaced. "I'll be grounded forever when she finds out."

"So, why did you decide to tell us?" Scarlett asked gently.

"I saw you come to help the tall man, and then your sister went for help. I thought the sheriff would solve the case, and we wouldn't have to tell anyone that we were here." The girl frowned. "Every day we waited to hear, but the only thing we knew was that the killer hadn't been found. Joe is still scared that the small man might find out about us."

Joe did look scared, but Althea was also acting more nervous the longer they were there.

Scarlett leaned towards them. "Telling the truth about things like this is very important, and I'm thankful that you trusted us. It will help a great deal."

"See, I told you we had to tell someone," Althea said haughtily to her friend.

Joe puffed out his skinny chest. "I was the one that said we should tell you, ladies, because you looked nice."

Violet grinned. "You're so sweet, Joe."

The boy flushed and studied his feet, while Althea made a rude noise.

"I don't suppose you saw what happened to the oar?" Scarlett asked, trying not to grin at the adorable pair.

"The small man took it with him when he ran up this path. He took the piece of driftwood too. It was big, and it must have been heavy because he couldn't run very fast. Once he got to the shrubs, we couldn't see which house he went into. "

The great information narrowed things down considerably and gave Scarlett an idea of where to begin the next phase of the search. "I don't want you to get in trouble for being late, but is there anything else you can tell us before you go?"

Althea and Joe frowned, then shook their heads.

"We don't remember anything else," Althea spoke on their behalf, and Joe didn't disagree.

By this stage, the sun was setting, so they began the walk back to Ruby and the other children at a slightly slower pace than on the journey here.

Althea plucked at a blade of grass and inspected it carefully. "We do know who the groom was."

Joe gasped.

"I don't want to lie," she told him. "It's not right."

"Weren't they too far away for you to see his face?" Violet asked gently.

"Yes, but he was so tall it had to be Chad Wood." Althea smiled. "He used to come and visit and play games with us."

Joe nodded. "He always brought treats."

The more she heard about Chad, the more Scarlett liked him. "And the other man? Was he familiar?"

"No. I couldn't decide who he was, but the man ran off in that direction." Althea pointed to the two houses in the distance, which were to the left of the path. "Most of the people from the big houses don't bother with us. Even the ones that aren't as clever."

When Scarlett and Violet looked confused, the child sighed before nodding at Lexie's house. "The Turners are the most important. Then comes the Woods. The other two are about the same as each other, although mom says that Mr. Whitley and his son are better carvers than the Johnsons. So, maybe they're not equal after all?"

It was shocking that in a short time, the hierarchy was revealed better by a child than all the adults involved. "Do all the sons learn the trades of their fathers?"

"Jobs? Yeah. That's how it works." Althea crossed her arms and scowled at no one in particular. "Except, I want to drive the trucks, and my dad says I can't."

Joe giggled, making Althea glare.

"I hope you get to do that, Althea." Scarlett smiled gently. "Now, we'd better get back."

The children nudged each other, and Althea took a bold step forward. "You had other things left in your basket."

Violet snorted. "Not much. We can take a look, and if there's nothing left, we could come back tomorrow and bring you both something nice."

Joe's eyes widened. "Nicer than cupcakes?"

"What if they were as nice?" Violet teased.

"No, they'd have to be better," Althea insisted. "We should get a reward for telling you everything, and that needs to be more than what the other kids got for doing nothing."

The kid had a point. "I'll make sure that whatever we bring will be the best thing you've ever tasted," Scarlett promised.

"Deal. Althea bounced on her toes. But can we still have what's in the basket?"

Violet laughed. "Of course. Let's go take a look."

Scarlett grinned. With her debating skills, and the ability to get Violet to agree to her demands, Althea should consider running for president.

Watching the other three run along the beach, she looked back to where the boat had been. Of course, there was nothing to see, just as on the day of the wedding, the soft sand would make it easy to cover footprints, but what had happened to the remaining oar?"

A shimmer of light hit the corner of her eye. The source appeared to be coming from a large deck of the house on the far left. A person stood, holding—binoculars?

If so, was it a casual observance, or was she the intended target?

CHAPTER 21

The picnic basket was empty. Not even crumbs lingered apart from the ones stuck to small faces, and Bob was doing his best to clean these too, eliciting giggles and feigned protestations.

The children lay enthralled on the rug with Ruby as she finished a story. Not only was her youngest sister in her element, but seeing Violet laugh as she chatted with Althea and Joe about what she would bring them, Scarlett couldn't remember the last time her family had look so relaxed and happy.

Given the circumstances, the irony wasn't lost on her, and she decided not to share someone may have been watching them. She'd hate to scare the children. Plus, she simply couldn't spoil the mood.

Ruby finished her story, and despite the disappointment of missing out on a cupcake, Althea and Joe insisted on helping to carry the stuff back to the van, and they'd said their goodbyes just as a mom came outside. The children scattered like blown leaves, and soon the street was empty.

Ruby sighed as she settled in the back with Bob, who

slumped in a heap at her feet. "That was a lovely picnic. We should do it more often."

"I agree, but we should come when the case is solved. I don't want the children to get into trouble by hanging out with us." Scarlett was already worrying about how Nate would handle this information. "Next time, we should introduce ourselves properly."

Ruby leaned forward. "Do you think they'll say anything about our visit?"

"They do seem to have a code amongst them for sticking together, which might delay things, but the young ones will be hard-pressed not to blurt something out," Violet mused.

"Their faces when they saw the cupcakes was precious, and when they tasted them, they were in raptures." Ruby chuckled. "I can imagine that they'd want to share that."

"It's nice to have our baking appreciated. Violet's smile was replaced by a frown. "How can we keep our promise of cupcakes tomorrow if we can't visit?"

"We'll find a way to get them here," Scarlett assured her, racking her brain to think of a solution.

"I couldn't tell by your faces, did you find out anything else when you went back to Turners' beach?" Ruby asked.

"We did." Scarlett gave her a quick overview. "Althea was a mine of information, and we have no choice but to tell Nate, but now I'm worried over how Althea's parents will react will."

"She'll really be in trouble for telling the truth?" Ruby gasped. "That's harsh when they're all such lovely kids."

"More likely for disobeying her parents in the first place." Scarlett was genuinely sorry that the children were in a tenuous situation through no fault of their own. The sparkle had gone from the day, so she gave them the last bit of news. "There is something else. While Violet walked back with

Althea and Joe, I saw someone with a pair of binoculars looking down at the beach from the Whitley's house."

"It's a long way from there. How can you be sure what they were looking at?"

"You're right, Vi, I can't. Only, I looked at those houses plenty of times while Althea told us her story. I'd swear that the balcony was empty before that."

Violet gave her a skeptical glance. "Good luck telling Nate that part."

Scarlett shrugged. "He's going to be annoyed with us no matter what we say, but I won't pretend that what I saw wasn't important to the case. I have to tell him what I think it means."

"He'll be expecting that, and you wouldn't want to disappoint the sheriff—it will only confuse him."

Scarlett glanced at Violet. "I can't believe you're teasing me."

"I can't believe you think I wouldn't. After all, it is Nate you're talking about."

Scarlett glanced at her sister. Something else was going on here that wasn't only to do with sisterly teasing. Violet was making a point, but what was it? "Look, I grant you that he's annoying, but he's still the sheriff. We have to show him respect."

"You're my sister, he's our friend, and we're no longer an item, so that makes it okay to tease both of you."

A sniff came from behind them.

"For goodness sake. Ruby, are you crying?"

"I can't help it, Vi. When you two are ribbing each other, it's like old times and makes me think of mom."

Scarlett reached over her shoulder and held one of Ruby's hands for a moment. Violet didn't look their way, but her hand joined theirs. The touching moment reminded Scarlett how important it was to enjoy life, just as their mom had. No matter what.

Soon enough, they'd be speaking to Nate, which would probably be less than enjoyable.

* * *

Nate burst through the door several minutes after Scarlett called him, which must mean he was already near. His mouth's tightness showed he was plenty mad at them for going to Harmony Beach, but he refrained from telling them what he thought while they told their story. And he wasn't the only one upset about the fact they could have been watched.

When they finished, Nate shook his head. "I can't believe you involved children."

Horrified, Scarlett protested. "It wasn't like that. They happened to be there, and one question led to another. They truly wanted to tell us, and I suspect it's been a burden that they've been scared to share with their parents or another adult."

"You should have called me before you went."

"You would have told us not to go," Violet reasoned. "We called you as soon as we got home."

"Which wasn't soon enough. I need to speak to those children." He handed Scarlett his notebook. "Please write down their names."

His coolness wasn't unexpected, yet Scarlett's mind went blank. She hated to go against him, but in this instance, she knew they'd done the right thing.

"It might be better for Ruby to do it," Violet suggested. "The children loved her, and I bet she remembers every name."

Ruby's mouth twitched into a soft smile. "They were adorable with funny little personalities and great manners. Bob adored them all."

Nate pushed the notebook across the kitchen table with a rumble of exasperation, and, in her neat handwriting, Ruby wrote down the names. Althea and Joe were rightly at the top.

Nate dragged his chair closer. "There aren't any last names."

Ruby glanced up. "They never offered them, and we didn't think to ask."

"Really?" Nate ran his fingers through his hair. "You didn't deem it important to the investigation like everything else you do?"

Suitably chastised, Scarlett intervened. "It shouldn't be an issue. The village is tiny with only twenty houses, so I doubt you'll have any issues with the names."

"I'll write the approximate ages and hair color which should help," Ruby offered.

"You won't harass the poor things, will you?" Scarlett wasn't above pleading.

Nate sat back, looking astonished. "That's not my style. Of course, if they choose not to talk to me, I will have to be firm."

Violet's eye narrowed. "They're kids, so they could be shy. In which case, you'll need to be patient."

"Shyness won't help me find a killer, and time is not on our side." Nate plucked the notebook from the table and put it in his pocket. "Stay away from Harmony Beach."

"You could at least say thank you," Violet retorted. "If we hadn't gone today, you wouldn't have an eyewitness."

"If you had informed me earlier, we wouldn't have children in potential danger," he snapped, as he marched out of their house.

"How rude!"

"He has a point, Vi." Scarlett conceded. "It never occurred

to me that we'd put them in danger until I saw the binoculars."

"You don't know for sure that's what they were," Violet argued.

"It doesn't matter if I imagined it—only that they're safe."

Ruby made a soothing sound. "Now that Nate knows he'll see to it that they are."

"With all my heart, I hope so." Scarlett rubbed her face with her hands. "We should fire up the laptop and search for any pictures of the Carvers. With a bit of luck, we might be able to figure out who the killer is."

Ruby collected it from the counter, hesitating before she opened it. "after what Nate said, do you think we should?"

"It can't hurt to look, and I imagine that Nate will have similar pictures to show the children." Scarlett reasoned.

It was growing dark outside when they unpacked the picnic things and cleaned up. Having dissected the entire experience several times, while viewing whatever they could find on the four families, the sisters were not much better off. There were several dark-haired men who might be the murderer, yet they had no way of being sure who was short or tall without the context of Chad being with each person.

Finally, Violet and Ruby headed to bed, leaving Scarlett to mull over the family trees she'd decided to produce. Something made her pull up a couple of pictures once more. There was something here. How had she missed the likeness?

Head bent when the light outside the back of the house went out, and she froze for a second. Her first rational thought was to lock the back door, but just as she reached it, the knob turned.

CHAPTER 22

L unging to throw all her weight against the door proved useless when the intruder pushed against it, her sock covered feet slipped along the wooden floor as if she were nothing more than an empty box.

"Miss Finch?" A voice hissed close to her ear. "Scarlett?"

"Who is it?" she managed through shaking teeth.

"It is Alex from the factory. Please let me in. I mean, you no harm."

Although urgent, his voice wasn't threatening, and he'd stopped pushing the door.

"I'm sure some part of you is already inside, and I don't remember issuing an invitation."

"I'm sorry to frighten you. When I saw you through the window, and you are alone, it was too great an opportunity to speak to you privately."

So he'd been watching the house. Was he also the person watching her around town? "I'm sure we could have worked out another way to meet. Perhaps another note?"

Alex made a sound that could have amusement, which would indicate he appreciated the dig at him about the note she'd received that had convinced her to accompany Nate out to the factory. At the very least, it confirmed that he was the culprit. Not that she had thought otherwise.

"It would be better for both of us for you to let me in and away from the lights." As he spoke, a large hand felt along the wall and plunged them into darkness.

Startled, Scarlett took a few steps back, which allowed Alex enough space to get completely inside and to shut the door behind him. Moonlight seeped in through the curtain-less window as she waited to see what he would do, hoping her instincts were right and that she and her sisters were safe.

Alex also stood quietly with his head tilted to one side in a classic listening pose. Nails clicked on the floor, and Bob appeared at her side, emitting a low rumble. Alex took a wary stance, unsure of Bob's nature when his people were threatened. It was a stalemate.

"What do you want?" she finally asked.

"Your dog is usually friendlier."

Scarlett ran a hand along Bob's back, and the dog sat. "He's as shocked as me that we have a late-night visitor and that we're all in the dark. About many things, it would seem."

"Dogs are sensitive to their people's feelings, and you are also very perceptive, Ms. Finch. Which is why I have come to you and not the sheriff."

She liked that he didn't say owner as so many people did. "Please take a seat, but be aware that George is also around somewhere."

"The cat? I wondered where he was." Alex looked about him and carefully sat his large frame in a chair.

Scarlett appreciated that he had the ability to decimate furniture and that he cared enough to be careful of hers. "Now, tell me why I am a better option than the sheriff or his men."

Alex put his hand out to the side, and Bob sniffed it before traitorously allowing the giant to scratch his head. She saw the gleam of his teeth.

"It surprised me that the Sheriff allowed you to be so involved in finding the killer."

Scarlett stiffened. "He didn't allow it. I do what I think is right."

"This is very noble yet dangerous. I have never met a woman like yourself."

Scarlett relaxed a little at the softness of his tone. Both things surprised her. "Did you stop by just to flatter me, because you could have done that during respectable hours."

Alex's eyes sparkled in the semi-darkness. "I am here because I believe someone has been bribed to delay the case or try to pin the death on another person—me."

She didn't let slip that Nate was already looking for the suspect the children had mentioned. "Our sheriff is too honest to allow that to happen."

Alex snorted. "He has men above and below him. They will not all think alike."

She nodded. It was something she'd wondered about but dismissed as unlikely. "The Turners might be powerful in their world, but Nate doesn't answer to them, and I'm sure he would do something if he thought other officers weren't being as professional."

"Something is delaying the process."

"You have to admit that you haven't helped. And there seems to be plenty of others at Harmony Beach with other agendas. In my opinion, that's the main reason the case has been so slow to resolve."

Alex stood and went to stand at the window where he could see out but couldn't be seen. "You are right. Again. It is difficult for me to discuss personal things with a stranger. Many at the beach feel the same."

Scarlett didn't doubt that but suspected it was more out of fear of losing their jobs and homes. The Carver's would have other worries—losing prestige or their positions in the hierarchy. "Shall I tell you what I know and what I suspect?"

He nodded. "That might be a little easier."

Scarlett closed her eyes, picturing the family trees and also a resemblance she'd previously overlooked. "You are Mr. Turner's son."

Alex hissed out a breath that told her she'd hit the nail on the head. It gave her the ability to continue to work through everything she knew, discarding the pieces of the puzzle which now couldn't fit.

"You should have inherited your father's position on the board, and you could have been the boss of the whole shebang."

"Shebang? I do not know this word, and how you came to this knowledge is a mystery, but I do not want to be the boss. The way the corporation is run is not fair to those who do the most work. However, how I feel does not matter. There are other reasons why I will never run this company."

Alex would be several years older than Lexie, and she could think of only one reason he couldn't run the company. A reason which an old-fashioned set of rules might leave no room for any changes. "Excuse me for being indelicate, but your parents never married, am I right?"

"Yes. I am sure you can appreciate that this matters a great deal to the corporation."

"Studying the workings of the corporation, I can see how that might be. Still, being accepted into the business must have been good for you?"

"Hah! Acceptance is a broad term. In my hometown, we were very poor and mistreated because my mother had no husband. I found out who my father was only after my mother's death when I went through her things. It took a long time to decide to contact him, and since he did not know I existed, he was as shocked as me. He sent money, and I came because I wrongly assumed I would be invited into the family. Instead, I had to pretend to be a distant relative."

"I'm so sorry, Alex. I didn't mean to stir up bad feelings."

He shrugged. "I have tried to accept my role in life, which isn't as bad as you might think. I'm tired of being a dirty secret, yet it is better to be here with food in my belly and a place to live."

"But, you shut yourself away."

"Not always. It is easier to be alone than to be looked down on. So I keep to myself at the factory, do a good job and visit the Carver Community who treat me well. They are more of a family than my own."

Scarlett saw his point, but the fact was he had more of a family than Mr. Turner. "Does Lexie know she has a brother?"

"I was sworn to secrecy. Mrs. Turner insisted on it if I was to remain in Harmony Beach."

"Ah, so she does know about you." Surprised for a moment, when Scarlett recalled the tenseness between Mrs. Turner and her husband, it was apparent that the marriage wasn't harmonious. You've done everything asked of you, but knowing who killed Chad, is too much to keep quiet about?" It was a guess, and maybe she couldn't see his reaction properly, but she witnessed the change in him as he slumped in the chair—the release of a long breath as if he'd held it for far too long.

"I didn't see it happen," he muttered.

"Alex, this is no time to get cagey. Do you know or not?"

He stood and paced the kitchen. "If they know I was the one to leak the information, I would be sent away. It's the only home I have."

"It would be a lie to say no one would find out because

once he's caught, you would have to testify against him, but it is the right thing to do. For Chad and Lexie and also for you. The burden is too much for an honest and fair man, and unless I am badly mistaken, I believe that's who you are."

He stopped and crouched in front of her. "This is why I am here. You want to make things right, just as I do, but it is dangerous."

Warring with her need to be honest and her promise to Nate, she placed a hand on his shoulder. "Two children from the community saw the murder. If they refuse to help Nate, the killer might be tipped off. We have to make sure they're safe, and we can only do that by catching him."

His head dipped, and when he looked up, the moonlight lit the anger on his face. "The person responsible is a miserable man. He is jealous of your friend and wants Lexie for himself. The board will not stand for either of them marrying her. Another has been chosen."

How Alex got his information wasn't important. The next target was. "Then, it's inevitable he will kill again. Sam might be his next victim, or it could be Lexie so that no other man will have her."

"I fear you are right. Over the last few years, I have watched her grow into a lovely woman, despite the treatment she endures." His fists clenched. "I will not let her or the children be harmed if I can help it. I heard of the families arguing without ever being in the house. They do not see the servants as real people and sometimes talk without realizing they are there."

Scarlett gripped his shoulder. "What was it about?"

"Any of the men from the other families were eligible to marry Lexie, but Chad was chosen as the eldest of the next prominent family. With him gone, his brother could be next in line."

"Your voice tells me that you don't believe he is the murderer."

He shook his head. "Michael and Chad were close, but Lexie and Michael were not. He and Ellen were about to announce their engagement."

Scarlett hadn't seen that coming. "Assuming that this is another arranged marriage, things could change?"

"They have been promised. Despite him not belonging to one of the two most prominent families, David Johnson will be the next in line. He will take the Turner name." Alex said this with a growl, and Bob jumped between them.

She rubbed his back, trying to come to terms with this. "That makes no sense. The old-fashioned way of doing things must make this hard for the other families to accept."

"I agree, but my father always gets his way. No matter who is hurt."

Scarlett shifted in the chair. Out of the muddle, the family tree came front and center. "David is in danger too. Because the killer is the one person who could never get to marry Lexie due to being the lowest on the rung."

"Joshua Whitley." They said the name together.

"Ellen's brother is a carver. He's short with dark hair and was missing at the wedding." Scarlett reeled off the list. "Ellen came to visit to find out what we knew."

Alex smiled. "You make an excellent detective."

Scarlett smiled back, knowing he had maneuvered her down the path to reach her conclusion, but it felt right. "We have to prove it first. I'm going to make coffee."

Before she could take more than a couple of steps, Alex threw her to the floor, and the kitchen window shattered simultaneously.

CHAPTER 23

G lass rained down on them.

Alex moaned, and his body jerked while she could only utter an "Ooof!" as the air was brutally forced from her body as the immense weight of Alex lay across her. "What the heck are you doing?" she gasped.

Ignoring her, Alex rolled to the side, pulling her with him, then he thrust her under the table. "Stay down."

Bob barked several times, and Alex issued a curt command. The dog whimpered and lay at Scarlett's back.

"I don't understand." She reached out to grip his arm, a warm stickiness on her fingers. "You're hurt!"

"Shush!" he hissed.

They lay together, his back toward the door. One long arm stretched to his boot, and he pulled a knife out and held it between them. Heart beating so hard it hurt, Scarlett stared into his eyes. Although he stared back, she fancied he didn't see her at all. Instead, he focused on listening intently to something she couldn't hear. Not that she'd hear anything above her labored breathing and the constant pounding of her heart.

After what seemed like an hour, he released her and rolled away to crawl to the door. She winced on his behalf, imagining glass fragments cutting through his jeans. And what about his injury? It had to be a gunshot wound. She hadn't heard a gun, but the glass breaking and then the sound of his pain followed by the blood pointed to that conclusion.

Light flooded the room, blinding her for a second. Alex muttered what surely must be a Russian curse before barreling out the back door.

"Hey!" Violet yelled as it banged shut. Then she was on the floor beside Scarlett. "Are you okay? What's been going on, and why is that man here?"

Tears misted Scarlett's eyes, and Violet held her close. "That was Alex. He's been shot. Someone fired into our house deliberately."

"At him or you?"

Scarlett swallowed her fear. "Right now, it doesn't matter. I need to phone Nate."

"I'll do it." Violet insisted.

"Okay, but stay away from any windows."

Violet crawled along to the house phone, and Scarlett followed her into the hallway. They sat on the floor their backs against the wall while Violet tapped impatiently on the handset. Bob wagged his tail, not understanding what was going on, and seeking reassurance. Scarlett put an arm around his neck, and he crawled onto her lap. He wasn't a small dog, but she didn't have the heart to push him off. Actually, she found it comforting to be in a little cocoon with Bob and Violet so close.

Meanwhile, her sister wasn't mincing words. "It's Violet. Someone shot at our house, and a man's been injured." There was little more conversation, and when Violet rang off, she put her arm back around Scarlett's shoulders. "Nate's on his way."

Scarlett shivered. "I guess having the sheriff's personal number is a good thing, after all." The attempt at lightening the mood fell flat in the face of Violet's terseness.

"It's his job, and I'm not about to wait for him to get here to find out what's going on."

A door opened down the hall, and Ruby came out of her room, rubbing her eyes. "People are trying to sleep." She stopped mid-way. "Why are you on the floor?"

Violet patted the floor beside her. "Turn off your bedroom light. Scarlett's just about to explain everything, and you should get down here too if you don't want to get shot."

* * *

Flashlights bathed the room, going backward and forward for a minute or two before Nate pushed the back door open.

"Is everyone okay?"

Before the women could answer, several shouts from outside caused Nate to retreat in a hurry. When he came back, the sheriff pushed a handcuffed Alex in front of him.

"Be a little gentler," Scarlett warned. "Alex is the one who's been shot, and he was looking for whoever did it."

Nate frowned. "Are you sure?"

Scarlett lifted her hands in exasperation. "He was here in the kitchen with me when it happened and saved my life by throwing me to the floor." She wasn't sure if this was true, or how he'd known it was going to happen, but was grateful that he'd been here.

"I need to sit," Alex said, stumbling to the table.

The women raced to his side, and Violet held out her hand to Nate. "Keys, please. He's about to faint, and I don't think any of us would be able to pick him up. Besides, we need to elevate his arm and put pressure on his wound to stop more blood loss."

Nate complied. Ignoring Violet's hand he unlocked the handcuffs himself. Ruby grabbed a kitchen towel and held it to the wound, and Violet brought Alex a glass of water. A deputy came to the door, and when Nate went to speak with him, Scarlett followed.

"We searched the property and found no one else. Shall we take the big guy to the station?" Deputy Glasson asked.

"He needs a doctor before he goes anywhere," Scarlett said firmly.

Nate nodded. "Sam should be here any minute."

She rubbed a temple. "Why, Sam?"

"I saw him coming back to town when I was heading here. Thinking it would be a lot quicker than calling the ambulance, I stopped Sam and asked if he'd come. Is that okay?"

Under Nate's scrutiny, Scarlett flushed. "Why wouldn't it be? I was just curious."

Nate raised an eyebrow. "Hmmm. I'd like you to go back inside just in case there's someone still out here."

She did as he asked, careful to keep out of the glass and went to check on Alex's injury. It looked as though the bleeding had stopped, and there was just time enough to make coffee before Sam gave a cursory knock and entered.

"Nate said you were all okay?" The question belied his concern as he searched their faces, lingering on Scarlett before his gaze eventually rested on Alex. "What are you doing here?"

"He came to see me." Scarlett wasn't sure why she felt the need to say this, but her tone had Sam shoot her a glance of surprise before turning his attention back to the injured man.

He lifted the towel and turned the arm both ways. "Looks like a gunshot."

Alex shrugged. "Just a flesh wound."

"It's a little more than that," Sam contradicted. "But the bullet went straight through, and it's a clean exit." He held up the towel, which was sodden. "Although it looks as if you've lost a lot of blood."

"He went after whoever did this, and we didn't get a chance to stop the bleeding until recently," Scarlett informed him.

Nate was close by, and he made a rude sound directed at the injured man. "Not smart when you had no gun. I need to look around the kitchen for that bullet. Carry on Sam, but if the rest of you could stand away from the windows, that would help."

"You should look around the table. We landed just in front of it."

Both men gave Scarlett a hard look, which was uncomfortable, although she couldn't say why. Forcing her features to remain neutral, Scarlett watched Nate cover every inch of the surrounding area. It must be frustrating since they were in the middle of a crime scene, and so many people had inevitably muddied it, but he doggedly checked and rechecked the area.

It was as he was crouched by the far chair that Scarlett noticed something by his head. Just under the table's overhang, a dark mark could be seen that she'd never noticed before. "Nate," she tapped his back. "Could that be the bullet?"

He swiveled quickly, knocking his head, then followed the direction of her finger. Frustration changed immediately to excitement as he pulled gloves from his pocket, and hurriedly slipped them on. A Swiss army knife was taken from another pocket to flick the bullet from the wood.

Scarlett wasn't bothered by the hole, and when Nate held open his palm, she was excited to see the squashed bullet. Surely this would prove who shot it. "Finally a break," she said as he slipped the bullet into a small plastic bag and tucked everything into yet another pocket.

Their eyes locked, and the rest of the room slipped out of focus for a moment.

"Thank goodness for that. Perhaps we could get a move on with any questions so we can all get to bed." Violet sounded snippy, and she shook her head at Scarlett.

What had just happened, and why was her sister put out about it? Scarlett forced her focus onto Sam's hands as he deftly cleaned, stitched, then wrapped Alex's arm. She'd run the gamut of all conceivable emotions and was suddenly bone-weary.

Sam was chatting to Alex and filling out his paperwork. "You've got good movement, so I don't anticipate any issue there, but you still need to go to the doctor or hospital tomorrow to get this cleaned and dressed. Are you allergic to any antibiotics?"

Alex shook his head. Some color had returned gradually to his face. "I do not think so."

Sam dropped a couple of pills into Alex's hand. "Take these now and another two tomorrow morning, then the hospital will issue you more."

"I will go there after work."

Sam frowned. "You can't work until this heals, and certainly no heavy lifting until the stitches come out in a week or so."

Alex didn't look pleased. "I suppose the gym is out too?"

Sam snorted. "Nothing strenuous outside of walking and fixing a meal. Now take the pills."

Alex sighed, but when Ruby handed him a glass of water, he threw the first two into his mouth.

"When Nate says you can go, I'll drop you home," Sam offered

"I have a car down the road."

"You're in no fit state to drive. We'll drop it off tomorrow," Scarlett offered.

He sighed again, fished around awkwardly in his pocket, and dropped his keys on the table. Then he pointed to the window. "Someone needs to board that up."

"I'll do it," Sam offered.

Scarlett shouldn't have been surprised as he'd always been good at doing handyman jobs for her, but that was before he'd admitted to being in love with Lexie. Now it seemed very wrong, and just having him in the house was uncomfortable. Naturally, Violet decided the situation was an opportunity to have Sam do penance.

"There's a sheet of plywood in the shed," Violet told him. "You'll find a hammer and nails there too."

To his credit, Sam ignored her harshness and left right away to get the wood. Meanwhile, Ruby swept up the glass while Nate continued with his questioning. Every aspect of the story was dissected several times until Scarlett's head spun.

Having covered the window, Sam took Alex home as promised. It took Nate a little longer to notice how bleary-eyed the Finch women were. Assuring them they'd be watched over, he also left.

The sisters took a few minutes saying good night, so it was after 1 a.m. when Scarlett got to be alone in her room. The quiet was a little unnerving. A deputy stationed outside eased her fears a little, but no matter how many questions she'd answered, there always seemed to be another to fill her mind.

If the shooter had wanted to hurt her, that meant he or she was perhaps a bad shot or was trying to frighten her off. If the target was Alex, was it a warning, or did the shooter want him dead?

CHAPTER 24

B ob snored softly beside Scarlett, who was wide awake. It occurred to Scarlett, before her eyes even opened, that George was absent for the whole of the evening. This was so unlike the large tabby who wanted to be at the center of everything that happened. And an awful lot had happened last night.

Slipping out of bed without disturbing the usually perky Labrador was a testament to how exhausting yesterday was for all of them. She threw on a dressing gown and padded barefoot to the kitchen.

To her relief, George was on his blanket near the door. "And where have you been, Georgie?"

He emitted a pitiful meow, which sounded like an apology and stood. Coming came toward her, he limped slightly.

"Georgie, you're hurt." She scooped him up as gently as she could, and he meowed some more and nuzzled her cheek. Something rubbed against her skin that wasn't fur. She lifted his chin and found a piece of material jutting from his mouth.

She held her hand out, and George dropped the fragment, smacking his mouth as if happy to part with it. "Did you hold onto this all night? Is it a clue to our visitor?"

He winked.

Scarlett peered out the unbroken window and saw deputy Glasson walking around the garden. She could call him but would prefer to speak to Nate about this. Plus, she needed to get George looked at by the vet. Placing him gently back on his blanket, she dropped the fabric on the table and fetched the cat some milk and a tin of salmon.

"You deserve a treat."

George sniffed the air appreciatively and wolfed down his breakfast in record time while Scarlett phoned Nate. It was early, but she was sure he wouldn't mind.

He didn't mind at all because he was on his way up the back steps. She opened the door and smiled. "I was calling you."

He held up his phone, where her name was displayed. "I see that."

"Were you on your way here?"

"I was in my car."

The way he said it made her think he didn't just arrive. "Don't tell me you were outside all night?"

He shrugged. "After I spent time at the station going through the evidence, I came back here in case the shooter returned.

Somehow that pleased her. "You must be shattered. I know I am, and I managed a little sleep."

"Deputy Glasson and I took turns patrolling, so it wasn't so bad. Did you want me?"

Scarlett didn't know what to say to the dark-eyed sheriff who was watching her in a way she'd never seen before. The silence was awkward until she remembered the material on the table. "I wanted you to know as soon as possible that George came home with something."

He followed her to the table. "What is it?"

"Maybe nothing, but I suspect it came from our would-be assassin from last night."

Nate's mouth dropped open. "Assassin?"

Scarlett raised an eyebrow. "Well, it could very well have been an assassination. If Alex hadn't been so darn quick, he or I could be dead right now."

"Even if that was his intention, how would George know to attack whoever it was and procure evidence? He's just a cat."

Nate's skepticism riled her. He'd seen George in action plenty of times and saying he was just a cat was—rude. "How does George know to do everything he can? Mable Norris must have taught him a few tricks, and you know how protective he is. George is special."

Nate took note of her hands on hips gesture, and his mouth twitched. "I agree that he's one clever cat, but why didn't he show up earlier with his—present?"

"He's injured. Maybe he needed to rest up, or perhaps he followed the perpetrator and only just got back. Although he could have been home for some time," she allowed. "The cat door allows him total freedom. I need to wake up my sisters so they can get to the café, and I can take him to the vet."

She also decided to take Alex his car but omitted to say so to Nate for no other reason than she wanted to talk to Alex alone. He seemed to like her, and she found him fascinating. It didn't hurt that he knew the four families of the Carver Corporation better than most. He was, after all, related.

When she saw George, Ruby was only too happy to help out once more, and Scarlett went to the vets as soon as she could.

Anita, the veterinarian, treated George gently and with

respect, but the tabby was unimpressed and refused to co-operate. The last visit had resulted in a routine shot, and George had a very long memory.

"George, let the doctor look at your leg. If you do, you can come for a drive with me."

Although he didn't look at Scarlett, he did allow Anita to manipulate his leg as she carefully examined it.

"Nothing's broken, but there is a little swelling on his thigh. My best guess is that he's fallen or been hit by something."

"Or someone," Scarlett muttered.

"Pardon?"

"We had an intruder at home last night. I think George was hurt trying to apprehend whoever it was."

Anita snorted, then quickly apologized. "Oh my gosh, I'm so sorry. That was unprofessional, and I can't deny that he's very smart—it's just that a sleuthing cat is not something you hear about every day."

Scarlett chuckled. "To be honest, I can't believe those words came out of my mouth, but the truth is George is not your average cat."

Either he understood that he was being praised, or was pleased not to be jabbed, because George began to preen himself with enthusiasm, purring loudly.

"I guess he agrees with you," Anita laughed. "Just watch him for a few days, and if the swelling doesn't settle down, I'll take an x-ray."

Carrying him to the car, Scarlett nuzzled the tabby. "I'm so glad it's not serious, and since you behaved, you get to come on a road trip, as promised."

She couldn't be too long because Ruby had to be at the library by nine at the latest, and it was a twenty to thirty-minute round-trip to the factory.

The place was bustling, with trucks coming in and out of the gates. Keeping clear of them, she drove the car around the factory and parked at the back away from the entranceway.

She didn't know where Alex's house or cabin was, so she headed to the reception area inside the main door. A middle-aged woman looked up and smiled.

"Welcome to the Carver Corporation. May I help you?"

"Is Alex available, or could you tell me where to find him, please?"

"Alex? Do you mean the night security guard? He won't be around at this time of day, and I'm afraid that we don't allow people to walk around the site due to security. It's a dangerous place out there."

She was pleasant if a little wary and Scarlett wasn't sure how to proceed.

"Is there a problem?" A man she recognized came out of an office close by and brushed past her.

"This woman," she looked apologetically at Scarlett, "I'm sorry I didn't get your name—is looking for Alex."

The man scowled, the recent looking shaving cut under his chin standing out. "Alex is not allowed guests on site."

"I'm not visiting. I'm returning his car." It was hard to stay calm when being studied like a bug a person might be inclined to stamp on.

"Why would you have it, Ms. Finch."

Her eyes widened. "You know who I am?"

"Certainly. I have a photographic memory, and you catered the wedding last Saturday."

He was arrogant, and Scarlett tried to picture which family he belonged to. He was working in the main office but dressed for the factory, so he must be a carver. Aka, a Whitley or a Johnson. She took a stab. "That's so nice you remembered Mr. Whitley."

He glared. "The death of my good friend is hardly something I could forget."

"You were close to Chad?"

"Very. Now, if you'll excuse me, I have work to do."

Scarlett made a show of checking her watch. "Good grief, I better get back. Thanks for your help." She hurried out the glass door and saw his scowling reflection as he watched her departure. These people were a sour lot, which made no sense when they had more than anyone she'd ever met.

No, what was she supposed to do? She climbed back into the car, and George gave her a dirty look. "I did say a drive, not a visit. And, since we can't find Alex, I guess we better go to the café."

George turned away, obviously still annoyed that she hadn't allowed him free run of the factory, but in a few seconds, he did an about-face. Coming across the seat, he sniffed the air around her, then her arm, before meowing loudly in her face. Next, he stood on her lap, searching outside the window and meowed disturbingly.

"What's the matter? What are you looking for?"

George continued to make a horrible sound, even after she'd settled him on the passenger seat and drove away from the factory. Just as she merged onto the main road at Harmony Beach, Nate came down the hill towards her. They both slowed, and when he came alongside, Nate signaled for her to pull over.

He jumped out of his sedan and ran across the road to where she'd parked. "I thought you were dropping the car off?"

"Apparently, he's not available during the day, and I wasn't allowed to search for him. Anyway, it occurred to me that I had no way to get back to the café. Hopefully, I'll catch up with Alex when he comes to see the doctor."

Nate nodded. "I'm glad you didn't try to look around by yourself. How's George?"

"Luckily, it's just some swelling. He'll be out chasing the bad guys again very soon."

It was meant to be funny, but Nate rolled his eyes, unable to appreciate how George was a cat version of Lassie.

"What brings you out here?" she asked pleasantly.

"I'm finally going to speak to the children in the village. Every time I've planned to do so, something crops up. And no, you're not coming with me."

"I couldn't, anyway. I have to get back to the café. Please ask Althea and Joe if they enjoyed the cupcakes Alex dropped off for us."

He touched the brim of his cap. "I will if I remember. You have a good day."

His smug expression implied that she didn't fool him. Of course, she wanted to go with him and ask a few more questions, but the café and Violet did need her. And Nate seemed delighted that she had other plans.

CHAPTER 25

The door was barely open when George launched himself out of the car and scampered, albeit with a limp, in the direction of the library. She didn't blame him. Spending time inside with Ruby had to be better than being left outside the café or at home by himself.

Snowed under with customers, Violet was relieved to see Scarlett, since Ruby had already left. After a brief catch-up regarding George, they worked solidly until well after lunch when they managed to drink a whole coffee and have a bite to eat.

Pulling a folder from her bag, Scarlett lay the copies Ruby had taken of the Carver photos on the table. Violet stood behind her.

"That's him," Scarlett tapped the face of the man she'd seen today. He stood in the back row while Chad sat in the front beside his father. "Joshua Whitley. I don't like him." She went on to explain her meeting with him.

"I don't recall him being at the wedding," Violet leaned down to get a better look."

"He said he was there, but since they all disappeared for a

while, it's hard to know if he came back or not. I guess Alex would know."

Violet slapped a hand to her forehead. "Oh, I meant to tell you that he phoned while you were attending to the knitting group. Alex apologized for not calling earlier. He was offered a ride into town first thing, and once the doctors check him, he's got a couple of errands to run but said he'll stop by later to pick up his car. I guess it was a wasted journey this morning."

"I was just thinking that meeting Joshua wasn't a highlight of today." Scarlett's jaw slackened as she visualized him. She'd been blinded by his dislike and pompous attitude. That shaving cut—could it be a deep scratch from an angry cat? A cat with a super snooper nose, who'd recognized a scent that lingered on her clothing.

A familiar and much welcome voice called from the counter in the café.

"Could I get a coffee?"

"Nate, come out the back," Scarlett called.

"I came to check you're all okay, but I don't want to discuss the case," he warned them as he entered the kitchen.

"Were the little children a little rough on you?" Violet teased.

"My guess is that they've been spoken to by their parents, and they clammed up like a, well—like a clam," he finished lamely.

"Nate, listen for a minute. I know what happened." Scarlett felt cogs slipping into place in her mind, and she wanted to get everything out in case it went away, or she missed something.

"Which particular time," he mused.

"I'm serious. When I went to the factory, I met Joshua Whitley. He knew who I was, yet we were never introduced.

He also has a fresh cut or scratch on his face that could have been caused by a cat."

Nate frowned. "You mean, George?"

"Precisely. And Joshua wore an overall. It was clean, and I saw no rip, but it was the same material that George brought me this morning."

Nate looked dubious. "Even if it's true, how do you propose we find a ripped overall in a place where that must be an everyday occurrence?"

Scarlett hadn't thought about that and fleetingly wondered if George could act as a sniffer dog. Maybe that was taking things too far. "How about a dog?" she said instead.

"It's a thought."

He didn't sound convinced that this was an option, and she felt a sliver of panic. "There's one more thing, and it's a good one."

"It always is."

"Sarcasm, Sheriff?" Violet scoffed.

Nate sighed. "It's the best I can do."

He did look tired, and Scarlett relented. "Joshua Whitley wore no ring."

Finally, Nate seemed to take her seriously. "Okay. I'll check it out as soon as I can. There's been a couple of crimes in Destiny, and my team's stretched."

"What if we ask Alex to help us?" Scarlett suggested. "I bet he knows his way around the factory better than anyone.

"I'll repeat this since you seem to be hard of hearing— there is no *us*. I will speak to Alex and see if he knows if Joshua was at the wedding the whole time and what their relationship is like." Nate made for the door.

"Alex is already helping," Violet retorted. "He saved Scarlett's life."

Nate hovered in the doorway, and though Scarlett wanted

to hit him with a cream cake for giving her such a hard time, she smiled. "You may as well stay for coffee. Alex is coming here to collect his car this afternoon, and he may have more to add."

"Would you like pie?" Violet asked sweetly.

Nate rolled his eyes and took a seat, no doubt hoping he wouldn't have to wait for long.

It was half an hour later when Alex walked into the café— with Lexie. Not sure what to make of it, Scarlett was grateful that no one else was about to witness her shock.

"Sorry to turn up like this." Lexie was pink-cheeked as she put her arm through Alex's. "I overheard my parents arguing last night and found out that Alex is my brother, which I believe you already know. I went to his place early this morning, and when I saw he was injured, drove him to Cozy Hollow. My parents don't know I'm here or that I heard them."

It almost sounded like she wanted them to keep this a secret, but the adoring look on Alex's face made Scarlett's insides warm. "You must have a lot to talk about."

He smiled. "I am still sad about Chad, but I cannot help being happy that I have a sister I can acknowledge."

Lexie sniffed. "I feel the same way about you."

"What are your plans?" Nate asked warily.

"We must get back to Lexie's home," Alex informed him. "There is a meeting about to take place where an announcement will be made concerning Lexie's future."

"How did you find out about this meeting?" Nate inquired stiffly.

"Lexie received a text."

"How convenient," Nate muttered.

"Will you come with us, Sheriff?" Lexie all but begged. It's going to get ugly when I refuse to accept their choice of another groom. Seeing me with Alex, who won't let me face them alone, won't help. I'm hoping the element of surprise will."

"I'll come and bring a couple of deputies, but what about Sam?" Nate asked.

Lexie blanched. "I haven't told him yet. I know he'll be mad, but I'd rather that than have the families attack him."

Scarlett could imagine how upset Sam would be. "What will happen after you confront them?"

"I have no doubt I'll be shunned, and I've made my peace with that. Chad and I should have stood up to them before." Lexie's eyes glistened. "I'm sorry for so many things, Scarlett. How Sam and I treated you wasn't fair, yet you've been nothing but kind to me. I wish there were some way to atone for the hurt I've caused."

Scarlett found the confession awkward, but even so, an idea pushed its way up and out. "There is something you can do. It might be dangerous."

"Anything." Lexie promised.

Scarlett looked to Nate. "You need more proof. I propose that we should all go and confront the group. They'll be in shock about Alex and also that Lexie would defy them. It might be the best chance to get the killer to show himself."

"This is a good suggestion," Alex agreed. "They cannot force Lexie to reconsider with so many on her side."

Nate ran his fingers through his hair, something he seemed to do with increasing regularity. "It could work, but there's no need for you to be there."

"I'm involved whether you like it or not. I want to see this through, and Lexie might need another woman by her side." She gave Lexie an imploring look.

Lexie nodded. "Please sheriff. Scarlett is so brave and inspires me to be the same."

Less enamored by Lexie these days, Scarlett kept her face bland while waiting for Nate's decision.

"I don't like it one bit." Nate fumed. "Okay. We'll go in my car, and you'll all do as I say." He pulled out his phone and organized his men.

Scarlett collected her bag. "I'm so sorry to leave you again, Vi."

"I'm keeping a tally," Violet said quietly enough for only Scarlett to hear. "Make sure you don't do anything stupid."

Kissing her on the cheek, she filed out the door after Lexie and Alex. Nate grabbed her arm and pulled her to one side.

"Being clever isn't the same as being smart. We both know things could get dangerous, so don't take any chances."

The look in his eyes held the warning, and something else she couldn't define. For the second time, she felt warm inside. "I'll be careful, Nate. Make sure you do the same."

He stared at her for a little longer before releasing her. "Let's go."

* * *

They discussed how to proceed on the journey, and when they arrived, Nate dropped them off at the end of the drive. It was a long walk, and they hurried, keeping close to the line of trees, which might afford them a little cover if someone were watching this way.

Lexie led Scarlett through the quiet house via the conservatory to the boardroom. Without knocking, she opened one of the heavily carved doors and entered. Scarlett stayed on her heels and experienced a sense of panic as they entered the darker room. All the chairs were taken except for one, and every pair of eyes focused on them.

"This is a family matter. Why is she here?" Mr. Turner boomed across the room.

"Because I want a witness." Lexie's voice broke a little, and she grasped Scarlett's hand.

"A witness? To what?" Mr. Turner scoffed. "You're being melodramatic as usual."

"To being bullied into marrying the next one of this bunch, you think suitable for your heir—since I am only a woman. Despite being more qualified than all of them."

"Silence!" Her father roared. "You will not speak to me this way."

"I will not be quiet when my future is in question, just as you wouldn't if this was about you. You're all so scared of change, of losing control of your empire, that you're allowing a murderer to remain free. Is that reasonable behavior?"

If she hadn't felt her shaking, Scarlett wouldn't doubt Lexie was anything but self-assured.

Murmurs came from the men at the table, and Mr. Turner scraped his chair back, his face like thunder. Only he didn't get to speak as just then, Nate came flying through the door, followed by Joshua Whitley.

Skidding to an ungraceful stop several feet in, the sheriff spun around. Joshua punched him squarely on the jaw. Nate reeled and fell to his knees.

Lexie clung to Scarlett, and they held a collective breath. Ugliness, steeped in hatred, shone through Joshua as he stood over the sheriff, hands fisted. His eyes fixed on Lexie. Wanting her as he clearly did, and watching her marry Chad must have unhinged him. Hearing that Lexie was to marry another of the group had sent him over the edge. He was practically frothing at the mouth with anger.

Joshua waved his gun around the room. "I'm sick of never being good enough for the rest of you. My family has been the better carvers and the backbone of this company since day one. Yet, we're treated like the bottom rung of a gold ladder because you decide that's what we're worth. Giving Lexie to Chad and now a Johnson makes me sick. Whatever you say, none of you are good enough for her, and I'm going to take the Corporation down once and for all!"

"You better shut your mouth if you know what's good for you."

Mr. Turner was a mottled red, and Mr. Wood wasn't much better. Scarlett was convinced that at this rate, someone would have a heart attack.

Mr. Whitley, pale and desperate, held out a hand to his son and pleaded, "Joshua, put the gun down before you hurt someone and end up in jail."

"If that's my only option, I better take it, because there's no way I'm going to live with the out-dated expectations you old men have."

Going worse than she'd imagined, Scarlett felt a prickle of sweat on her neck as a massive shadow appeared at the doorway.

CHAPTER 26

"Give me the gun." Alex's voice boomed across the room. "What are you doing here?" Joshua wasn't the only one confused.

"Saving your life. Not that you deserve it."

"Don't say that," the younger man begged. "You and I are friends."

The other men appeared shocked by this admission, and frankly, so was Scarlett.

Alex grimaced. "Killing Chad, who was a true friend to everyone, changes everything. Naturally, I wasn't invited, but I watched the wedding from above the beach. You thought no one was around to notice where you went. And friends don't shoot each other."

Joshua paled. "What are you talking about? Who did I shoot? And I've seen you since the wedding, and you never mentioned any of this. You're only guessing it was me."

"I saw you head in the direction of your house and assumed you wanted to be alone. Knowing how upset you were about the marriage, I should have followed you. That might have changed everything."

Alex's tragic look didn't move Joshua.

"You're bluffing. Other people were missing that day."

The gun was now pointing at Alex, and Scarlett took a step forward. "We have other witnesses who say that instead of going home, you took the walkway to the beach."

Joshua waved the gun at her, then the rest of the room's occupants, before settling once more on Scarlett. "Why couldn't you stay out of my business?"

Nate stepped in front of Scarlett and held out his hand. "You killed a man. That makes it everyone's business. Let me take the gun before you make another mistake."

"Chad was a good man," Alex reminded Joshua. "He was your friend—your family. There is no excuse, but speaking the truth might stop another tragedy."

"Please, son," Mr. Whitley begged.

The other board members huddled against the far wall, distaste apparent as Joshua crumpled, literally. It started with his mouth and flowed down his body until he knelt on the floor. Alex leaned down to pluck the gun from limp fingers and then handed it to Nate, with such a sorrowful look, tears prickled Scarlett's eyes and made the room blurry. Ejecting the bullets, before tucking the gun in his belt, Nate withdrew his handcuffs as two deputies stepped inside the room.

"Is that necessary?" Mr. Whitley exclaimed.

"I'm afraid it is," Nate said firmly.

"I'll come bail you out as soon as they let me, son."

Nate shook his head at Scarlett's quizzical look. There would be no bail for Joshua. No matter the motive, Killing Chad with an oar couldn't be construed as manslaughter. She imagined that Joshua would spend a considerable amount of time behind bars. However, it was good to see Joshua's father trying to make him feel better or give him hope.

Lexie made her way closer to Joshua, her cheeks wet. "How could you kill Chad?"

"You didn't love him, and he didn't love you. But I do." Anguished, Joshua pleaded for Lexie to understand. "We could have been so happy."

"Your actions aren't about love." Disgust dripped from her words, and Joshua flinched. "You're just like your father and the others. When will any of you understand that a woman is not your property to manipulate like a chess piece and that nobody in this room was half as good as Chad."

"Lexie now is not the time for hysterics," Mr. Turner dismissed his daughter.

She stood firm. "I'm not hysterical, merely speaking the truth, at precisely the right time—while you're all here, feeling sorry for yourselves, and before you can regroup and put the rest of us under your elitist and sexist thumbs. I will not spend any more of my life being miserable like most of you are. And, in case there's any doubt, I refuse to marry anyone you suggest—ever again." Lexie took a deep breath. "I love Sam, and we're going to leave town unless you find a way for the women in our families to have a say in our lives and the company.

"Don't be ridiculous," her father blustered. "That's not how these things are done, and you will do as all the others before you have done. The paramedic is not one of us."

He wasn't the only one who looked ill or outraged at the prospect of women having a say, and Scarlett's anger threatened to spill out, but someone else got there first.

Alex slammed a meaty fist on the boardroom table. "Enough! It is time to change."

Mr. Turner paled. "Alex, I appreciate you have an opinion, and that you helped just now, but this is none of your concern."

The injustice of Alex's opinion being more important than his daughter wasn't lost on Scarlett, and though Lexie also looked unimpressed, Alex was on a roll.

"Do I not work for you? Haven't I done everything you asked?" he insisted.

"Exactly—you work for me," Mr. Turner agreed. "Any changes will be discussed with the board, and I will let you know what they are later."

"No. Everyone deserves to have a say, and there is never a good time for you to listen. I am your eldest child, and that will no longer be a secret. You will listen, or I will leave too."

Alex's voice filled the room, and Mr. Turner clutched at his chest.

"What is he saying?" Mr. Johnson asked. "I thought he was a distant relative brought over here when his mother died."

Alex shrugged. "That is what I was told to say when my father brought me here."

Mr. Turner gasped. "You promised not to say anything."

"That was before I knew how cruel you are," Alex scoffed. "I was poor, but I had a life in Russia. Hidden like a dog, I have no life here. It didn't bother me when I was younger—now it does." He glared around the room. "When you found out about me, you decided to bring me into your life, but not as a real son. Now I have a sister who is not bothered how I came to be, and we are happy to have each other."

Mr. Turner turned to Lexie, perhaps hoping for a show of loyalty, but his daughter refused to meet his gaze. She was looking at Alex—with love. Brother and sister stood side by side—united.

Scarlett could see it was how she felt about Ruby and Violet. Maybe there was a silver lining after all.

"I do not like how these people treat the workers," Alex continued. "It is bad enough that they do not like each other and have forgotten how they came to be so powerful, but fathers and sons fighting and hurting each other, that is too much. As Lexie said, Chad was too good for this company, and thanks to Scarlett, I finally see that keeping quiet does nothing good."

Even the prisoner was wide-eyed with shock, and though she now had every eye on her, Scarlett tilted her chin. She couldn't have said it better than Alex and greatly admired his courage, even if it did make her many enemies. He gave her a small bow, and his persistent scowl disappeared to be replaced by a soft smile. It transformed his features as if a significant burden had fallen from his massive shoulders.

Living in a state of envy and unhappiness, these families had lost sight of what was truly valuable. But Alex understood that what they really needed was right in front of them all along—family. Instead, they were bound by fear and harsh rules that didn't allow for independent thoughts or feelings. Could they hear and possibly accept his words?

"Freedom is important." Had she said that aloud? It appeared so.

Lexie stood beside her. "All kinds of freedom. Hearing many times about our ancestors' struggles, you would think that would mean something to you. Just because a rule or decision was made decades ago isn't a good enough reason to continue it."

Scarlett gazed around the room, hoping to see a glimmer of something that might hint at a change of heart.

After a long silence where the rest of the group looked unable to come to terms with the news of Alex or the forthrightness of Lexie, Nate handed the accused to Deputy Glasson.

"I think we've all had enough for the moment, but there will be more questions to be answered, so no one should leave Harmony Beach. Alex and Lexie, would you come with me? We'll need your statements."

Alex nodded, and Lexie did the same, while their father scowled in the background.

Scarlett decided that anywhere would be preferable to this house, even the station. She followed the group, done with trying to talk sense into these people.

"He isn't one of us. His opinions don't matter," Mr. Johnson yelled after them.

Continuing to walk down the hall, Nate had the last word. "Be assured—they matter. To the courts and me."

They nearly made it to the front door when Mrs. Turner hurried down the stairs, stopping near the bottom.

"I heard yelling. Where are you going, Lexie? What's happening, and why is that man with you?" she nodded distastefully at Alex.

"I have no idea if you knew that Joshua killed Chad. However, I believe you know that Alex is my half-brother," Lexie said bravely.

Her mom reared back, clinging to the stair rail for support. Seconds later, her eyes resembling flint, she straightened. "I know who he is. That was not my question."

How hard had it been for her to accept her husband's child? The answer was pretty clear to Scarlett—she hadn't accepted it at all.

Lexie stiffened. "He was here to explain who killed Chad. Now we're going to the station to give statements."

"Does your father know the two of you are leaving together?"

Scarlett couldn't believe the woman wasn't focused on who the murderer was or at least a little worried at how Lexie must feel about a brother who'd been kept from her.

"He does, and he's not happy," Lexie admitted sadly. "But that can't be helped."

Mrs. Turner arched an eyebrow. "Are you coming back when you're done?"

Was that a touch of fear in her voice?

"I'm not sure." Lexie shrugged. "I guess that depends on you and dad."

Lexie left it at that, but Scarlett thought she detected a touch of admiration in Mrs. Turner's face.

Perhaps all was not lost.

CHAPTER 27

The sheriff's department was a hive of activity for this time of the evening. Cozy Hollow had less than its share of drunks, crime, and few fatalities, except natural causes—until recently.

Joshua was taken downstairs to the cells by Deputy Glasson while Nate led Lexie and Alex to an office Scarlett had never been inside. Tagging along, because they'd all come in the same car, her eyes were drawn immediately to a framed medal gracing one wall along with a newspaper clipping she would have liked to read. There were also a couple of what she imagined were family pictures on the desk, that she couldn't fully see.

"Please take a seat." Nate sat behind the sizeable tidy desk. "I'm sure today was harrowing for all of you. I want to thank you for helping me solve this case, and your statements will make sure that justice is served."

Alex hung his head, and Lexie studied her fingernails.

Scarlett's throat burned. Justice did need to be served, but Joshua was not the only party suffering from guilt. "What Joshua did was awful and deserves punishment, but I can't help thinking that he's mentally unbalanced and a product of his environment. Is there a chance that Joshua could get psychiatric help?"

Nate looked perplexed. "That's not for me to say."

"Please don't worry about him, Scarlett. My father will make sure he's taken care of, regardless of what he's done." Lexie said wearily. "Sometimes, the corporation works as it should."

"Perhaps they might build on that and let women on the board one day," Scarlett said hopefully.

"Rebecca, Ellen, and I talked about it from time to time. In fact, Rebecca was angrier about how things worked than I was. It was her suggestion for Chad to take the Turner name in the hopes that Chad could make some changes. Of course, her father took the credit for the idea."

Scarlett's mouth dropped open. "Rebecca? The one in love with Chad?"

Lexie smiled. "We were all a little in love with Chad."

"Sam said that Rebecca and Chad loved each other." Scarlett was already thinking about the possibility that Joshua had an accomplice, if not in the murder, then certainly in the cover-up.

"I think I would have known that," Lexie insisted. "I'd like to get my statement done, Sheriff."

Nate coughed and shook his head at Scarlett when he saw she was going to continue with her questions. "I'll get coffee and see if we can get that process started."

The second he left, the silence was deafening and, therefore, awkward. Lexie was clearly not as observant as she thought, but Nate seemed to be aware of this already, so Scarlett didn't belabor the relationship.

"What do you intend to do afterward?" Scarlett asked. "You talked about leaving town with Sam."

Lexie shrugged. "Sam and I have spoken about it. That

was before I knew about Alex. Now that we've found each other, I'm not as sure I can up and leave."

"I feel the same way," Alex added.

"I do know that I don't want to go home," Lexie added. "Seeing my father will only drcdge everything up, and I don't hold any hope he will change."

"If you need a place to stay, I could ring the hotel for you," Scarlett offered.

Lexie's mouth quivered. "After all I did, I can't believe how kind you are. It was you who solved the case, and I know I didn't help as much as I should have. I feel so bad about so many things."

"Nobody spoke up," Alex said softly. "We all must carry the guilt, but we can't change what has happened." He turned to Scarlett. "I can't go back there, so I would appreciate a room."

"It's no trouble at all. If there's none, then you can sleep on our couch, Alex, and we'll find room for you if you change your mind, Lexie. Unless you'll be staying with Sam."

Lexie reddened. "We've never spoken about living together."

That should have meant something to Scarlett. Surprisingly, it didn't.

Alex took Lexie's hand. "You have a man who loves you, and there is no shame in loving him back."

"It would be a shame to have Chad's death mean you can never be happy with Sam. I don't think he'd want that for either of you." Scarlett took a pack of tissues from her bag and handed them to Lexie, who wiped her face and managed a watery smile.

"It feels too soon to talk about this, but thank you for your generosity."

Running footsteps came down the hall, and Sam burst into the room just as Alex pulled Lexie into a hug.

"What's going on?" he yelled.

The shock on his face was priceless and somewhat ironic, considering how Scarlett felt when she'd realized that Sam was in love with Lexie. Sam had no clue about the latest events, and Scarlett snorted before she could stop it.

Lexie lifted her tear-stained face and met Scarlett's gaze. She blushed, then sighed resignedly. "Sam, let me introduce my brother, Alex. We've left home and need a place to stay."

Sam was stunned for a while longer, and feeling suddenly out of place, Scarlett stood.

"It's been a long day. Actually, it's been a long week. I'm going home. Nate knows where to find me. Good luck, everyone, and don't be a stranger, Alex. I owe you my life, and you're welcome at the café anytime for free meals."

He grinned. "You wouldn't say that if you knew how much I eat."

"Hah. Violet might give you a run for your money."

He looked confused, but she didn't have the energy to explain. There would be enough of that when she got home.

CHAPTER 28

Sitting on a rug on the back lawn, enjoying a lazy Saturday morning, Scarlett was surrounded by the people who mattered the most to her. She tilted her head, enjoying the summer sun on her face and a peace that she'd missed. Watching her every movement, Bob gave her cheek a sloppy kiss, which made her laugh.

Olivia handed her an iced tea. "That dog adores you, and George is your next biggest fan. I never saw that coming."

"I'm so lucky to have these guys in my life." Scarlett agreed. "Present company excepted, I've concluded that I have no idea about men. Perhaps it's easier to enjoy the life I have and stay single."

"You're not alone there," Violet agreed from beside her. "Are you still upset about Sam?"

Scarlett stilted her head towards her sister. "There's been plenty of time to think about what he did, and I honestly believe his intention wasn't to hurt me. He couldn't have Lexie and was, therefore, determined to make our relationship work."

Violet frowned. "That's incredibly big of you, but I'm still upset that he loved another woman the whole time you were together."

Scarlett understood how Violet felt. With many hours lost reflecting on Sam's betrayal, she'd worked her way through it and realized that she should have been hurt for longer—less embarrassed—angrier. It was time to confess.

"If I'm honest, it was my pride that took the biggest hit. Naturally, I'm sad that it happened, but what was Sam supposed to do—be single for the rest of his life? He tried hard to be the perfect boyfriend, and I'm sure he would have continued to do the best he could. How could he have known what would happen with Lexie?"

Violet shook her head in wonder. "You're more gracious than I could ever be. They would always have been around each other because of Sam's friendship with Chad. And by default, you would have been too. That wouldn't have been easy for them, but imagine if you'd gotten married and then saw them making eyes at each other!"

Ruby tutted. "There's no point in imagining. It's a shame Sam couldn't have been honest, but his best friend is dead and who's to say if he and Lexie will be happy together after all this history."

Olivia, the only one to sit in a chair, sipped her iced tea before pulling her hat a little lower, to protect her face from the mid-morning sun. "How could Sam ever broach the subject? *My dear, Scarlett. I would like to be your boyfriend if you aren't bothered by me loving Lexie.* Being sensible can help get your mind around all sorts of situations, but it will never stop most of them from happening."

Scarlett appreciated her aunt's words. "In a way, it reminded me of what's important and made me realize that I wasn't truly in love with Sam. Not the way I should be. I wanted to have a boyfriend and thought that what we had was good enough. I'm relieved neither of us had to put that to the test."

Violet nudged her. "You already have a love—the café."

Scarlett kissed her forehead. "And also, my family. I know you're going to leave as soon as you can, Vi, but we'll always be there for each other. It won't matter where you go or what you choose to do—boyfriends or husbands aren't going to change that. We are not the Carver Corporation."

Violet grimaced. "Thank goodness! Anyway, you might like to know that I've decided what I want to do."

Scarlett ignored the prickle of loss. "Really? That's wonderful."

Ruby rubbed her hands together. "Finally. What is it?"

Violet drew out the moment by sipping her tea before grinning. "I'm going to train to be an assessor, like Phin. When I went to Portland with him to sell our book, I felt—alive."

"I knew you relished being involved that way, just as I know you'll be great at it. You can stand up to anyone, and no doubt, you'll get the best prices for your clients." Scarlett had to say these things, even though having her sister leave home would be a wrench that she wasn't quite ready for.

Violet, as usual, saw through her. "Except you. I can never best you."

"What do you mean?" Scarlett asked.

"Any time I threatened to leave or mentioned that we should sell the café, one look at your face, and all my resolve slipped away."

Scarlett grinned. "I'd say I'm sorry, but that's not entirely true. Thanks for sticking by me. Without you and Ruby, The Cozy Café would have been long gone."

Violet smiled. "We knew how much it meant to you and Mom. We did what was right at the time."

"And times change." Scarlett took Violet's hand. "I know

I've said this so many times, Vi, but I'm seriously going to spend every spare minute looking for your replacement at the café. I promise."

Bob leaped from Scarlett's lap and bounded to the corner of the house just as Nate appeared.

"Good grief, Bob, you've put on some weight," he laughed.

"Welcome, Sheriff. To what do we owe the pleasure of your visit," Olivia asked.

"It's more of a courtesy call. Rebecca has confessed to her part in the cover-up."

Scarlett raised an eyebrow. "And of shooting, Alex?"

Nate groaned. "Yes, you were right."

"You never told us that," Violet scolded.

"Since I told Nate the other night of my suspicions, I've been trying not to think about it. Alex said Joshua was a bad shot, and it occurred to me that he couldn't possibly have hit Alex if he was so bad. Nate looked into the local gun club, and Rebecca turns out to be a crack-shot."

"What you don't know is that when we searched her house, we not only found her gun which the bullet matches, but we found both the oars and traces of blood and hair on one of them."

Scarlett smiled. "I appreciate you coming to tell me. Case closed and no more questions. The day gets better every minute."

"Maybe we could go out one night to celebrate?" Nate said, suddenly looking nervous.

"All of us?" Violet asked.

"Oh. Yeah. Sure."

"Lovely," Olivia said with a saucy wink.

Nate wore a pained expression. "Great. I'll be in touch."

He'd barely disappeared around the side of the house when Violet laughed, and Olivia joined in.

Scarlett laughed too until she realized they were laughing at her. "What's so funny?"

"You are," Violet sniffed. "He was asking you out."

"Me? As in a date? No way!"

"He absolutely was," Olivia insisted.

Scarlett didn't know how to react, and her stomach was doing funny things. "That's terrible if it's true. Vi, I had no idea he liked me that way. Is that why you've been so angry with him?"

"I've been angry because he was trying so hard to prove that he didn't prefer you to me. I told you ages ago that I didn't want Nate as a boyfriend, but he'd be perfect for you. Plus, I hinted at him liking you, and I told him what I thought about it. He denied it, which only made me madder."

Scarlett recalled a couple of times when that might have happened. "I thought you were teasing me."

"Which is why I didn't say anything outright. I wanted you to find out under your own steam how you felt about him—when you'd gotten Sam out of your system once and for all. He gets points for being brave enough to ask you out in front of us." Violet smirked.

"Ruby, is this true?"

"It is, and you should go on that date without us." Ruby's eyes twinkled merrily. "If you want to."

"I'll have to think about it. I'm so confused." Scarlett confessed.

"Well, just to change the subject, I have something to add about a new employee for the café. Look no further."

All eyes swung to Olivia.

"Do you know someone who'd be interested?" Violet asked excitedly.

"If you don't mind that I'm not as clever in the kitchen as any of you, then I'd like to help out. I could cover for Violet fulltime as an interim measure until you find yourself an apprentice, then I could work part-time at the café and do a few hours at the craft shop."

It sounded as though Olivia had thought this out in great detail, but Scarlett couldn't understand the reasoning. "What about Cozy Crafts? You can't possibly run it on a part-time basis."

Olivia shrugged. "I had an offer last week, a fair one, that I couldn't refuse, from a group of women. It will be good for Cozy Hollow, and besides, it's time to move on."

"No way! Your store is part of the town's history. If you're struggling financially, we can help out." Ruby gave Scarlett and Violet a pleading look. "We have some money left from the sale of the book."

"Of course," Scarlett agreed, while Violet nodded vigorously.

Olivia waved a hand at them. "As kind and generous as your offer is, I must decline."

"Please let us fix this," Ruby begged. "You love that shop."

"Yes, I do. Only not as I once did. Don't get upset about this because now that I've made the decision, I'm happy about it. The shop is a lot of work for one person, and book-keeping was never my strong suit."

Ruby wasn't buying it. "But I could do your books. Or, Scarlett, if you prefer."

"I'd be happy to," Scarlett agreed while noticing that Olivia was incredibly calm about making such an enormous decision.

"Your lives are just getting sorted, and I won't be a burden on my favorite nieces, so stop asking me to," Olivia chuckled.

Violet laughed. "Aren't we your only nieces?"

"True, but let's not let the facts get in the way of a good story, dear. Plus, I don't want you to feel sorry for me." Olivia winked. "I'll come out with a nice little nest egg. I might even travel."

"How did this come about?" Ruby demanded. "And why didn't you tell us that this was even an idea?"

"Goodness, it's like twenty questions. I didn't say anything because I wasn't one hundred percent sure. Working at the wedding made my mind up about whether I could fit in at the café and concluded I could. Like the three of you, I'm stubborn and didn't want to be hired out of pity or just because we're related. Now, do I have a job or not?"

The sisters looked at each other questioningly, and after a moment, they all nodded.

Scarlett grinned. "You're hired. When can you start?"

"In a month if that suits? First, I have to get my books in order and see my bank manager and then my lawyer in Destiny."

"Sounds perfect to me." Violet was practically bouncing off the rug, and Violet never bounced. "I better give Phin a ring and see when I can begin my training."

"Lucky we're used to shocking news and upheavals," Ruby teased.

Violet laughed. "Lucky we have an aunt who wants a change of occupation."

Scarlett groaned. "I just thought, if you're at the café every day, we'll never get rid of the knitting group."

"There is that," Olivia agreed. "But I'll make them buy something every hour; otherwise, they can hit the road."

"You can't do that," Scarlett protested.

Olivia waggled her eyebrows. "Just you watch me."

She was so much like their mom that Scarlett's throat constricted. Just when life seemed to head one way, it laughed in your face and went in the opposite direction.

Still, the unknown wasn't always a bad thing, and right at this moment in time, Scarlett wouldn't want to be anywhere but here with her family. Including, Bob, who was now lying across her feet, and George, who lay behind her shielded from the sun by her shadow.

For someone who'd professed not to be a cat-lover, she'd been converted quite quickly, and not wanting any more pets had proved futile because Bob had also decided she was his person.

It was a funny world, indeed. And about to get more interesting.

Olivia casually sat forward to refill their glasses. "I forgot to mention that I saw Harvey on my way here. He's had an offer to lease the diner."

"But the rebuild has only just begun," Ruby protested.

Olivia's eyes twinkled. "The new person is not in any hurry and prepared to wait until he can move in."

"He? Do you know who it is?" Scarlett asked warily. The glint in her aunt's eyes meant she was about to spring big news on them.

"It's not often I hear something before you, dear, and you will certainly be surprised." Olivia paused for effect. "It's Alex."

Scarlett almost dropped her glass. "He can cook?" She'd seen Alex once since the end of the case, but as he and Lexie had ended up staying with Sam, the conversation had proved awkward.

Olivia winked. "The man has many talents. I'm so glad he's staying around. He'll be a wonderful addition to Cozy Hollow's list of eligible bachelors."

Scarlett sighed, wondering if having Olivia around every day wouldn't be playing right into her aunt's match-making hands.

Was it too late to back out of the job offer?

~~~

Thank you so much for reading Mocha Mayhem. Book 4 is in the works, meanwhile, you might like to try The Maple Lane Mysteries.

Madeline Flynn, aka Maddie, lives in a small town on the other side of Destiny. Her path may cross with Scarlett in the future, but for now an **Apple Pie and Arsenic** excerpt is on the next page

APPLE PIE AND ARSENIC

Have you read the Maple Lane Mysteries yet?

Madeline Flynn came home to Maple Falls to look after her beloved Gran. It looks like it was all a ploy, yet the chance to own her own bakery is too tempting to walk away from.

Excerpt:

Maddie could smell the pie from where she was standing, and Bernie had a hopeful glint in his eyes. Once you'd tried Gran's baking, nothing ever tasted as good. People came from miles away, paying her to make birthday cakes and delicious baked treats, and had done so for years. More often than not, she took less money than she should, and it was agreed by all her customers that whatever treat she made and whatever she charged was certainly worth it.

Bernie opened the back of his van and carefully pulled out a large cage and set it on the grass beside the driveway. Once he'd taken her bag to the porch, Maddie gave him his fare and added a hefty tip for his trouble. Not everyone wanted a cat like hers in their vehicle, but Bernie never raised an eyebrow, and he always did the lifting, which was a marked difference from New York City cabbies.

"Just you wait a minute," Gran said to Bernie.

He grinned in anticipation. No-one went away from here without something to eat.

Then she gave Maddie a hug. They hugged hard, the way Maddie had been taught. The Flynn mantra was "Hug someone like you mean it, or don't bother."

She savored the smell of apples and cinnamon, which was Gran's brand of perfume. One that couldn't be bought. One that meant love and home.

Gran smiled, a little misty-eyed, when they let go and went inside to fix a plate for Bernie.

Big Red yawned as Maddie opened his cage, then jumped out onto the grass as gracefully as he was able. "I'll be inside," she told him, giving his arched back the expected scratch.

The big Maine Coon gave her a disgruntled look, stretched, and with a flick of his tail sashayed over to the shade of the maple tree that dominated the front yard.

Poor boy. She could appreciate that his trip had been a great deal less comfortable than hers. Even with the air conditioning on, the taxi had been hot, and what the plane had been like for him, she hated to think. He wasn't a cage kind of animal, and he would only get into it with great reluctance and many treats.

For such a short visit, she would ordinarily leave Big Red with her roommate, but she was currently without one thanks to a monumental argument. Apparently, Maddie shouldn't be upset over said roomie and Maddie's boyfriend enjoying more than friendship while she was away at a baking contest. Dalton's agreement that she was overreacting still reverberated in her head, and if she was truthful, she was glad to escape the drama.

The kennels had let her know last time that Big Red wasn't welcome back—something to do with asserting his authority overzealously with his peers.

Trying to make the proverbial lemonade with this bunch of lemons had drained her well of optimism.

Gran came out with the covered plate and handed it to Bernie who looked as excited as a child at Christmas. "I'll expect that plate back next time you're passing," she said.

"Much appreciated and I will." He touched his cap and carried it carefully back to his car as if he held precious gems.

"Welcome home," Gran called out to Big Red. She gave a wry smile as Maddie joined her on the porch. "He looks cross. I guess he'll come in when he's ready."

"You know him so well." Maddie grinned. "Now, tell me how you really are. I've been so worried since your call. I'm sorry it's taken a couple of weeks to get here."

Gran waved her apron at the fuss. "I'm doing great, and I'd have been pleased to see you any time you could make it. I certainly didn't expect you to be on the next plane."

Maddie had thought Gran might resist her help when she'd called to say she was on her way home. When no resistance was forthcoming, she'd assumed the worst. "I'm so glad you're doing a lot better than I was anticipating."

"Goodness, did I give the impression I was on death's door?" Gran chuckled. "The bronchitis was bad, but the cough's nearly gone. Although, I do admit that the packing seems to have made me a little maudlin."

Maddie put an arm around her as they walked through to the kitchen, leaving her bag for later. "It's only natural. This is your home, and you've lived here all your life."

Gran squeezed her waist. "Like you."

They were the same height of 5'7" and had similar builds.

When Maddie looked at pictures of her childhood and compared them to Gran's, they looked so alike that they could have been sisters. For a child without parents, that was a big deal.

"Yes, that's true, but I've also lived other places now. Not that I won't shed a tear or two when you sell, but I'm sure it won't be as painful for me as it will be for you."

"That you understand means a great deal to me, sweetheart. I sure hope you don't mind using your vacation time to help me out. I hate to be a bother."

"Pssssh! You could never be a bother, so don't give it a thought. Where else would I take a vacation? Plus, I wouldn't have let you do this by yourself. Real estate agents can be hard to deal with, and you'll want to get a good price."

"I know you don't take nearly enough vacation time, but I'm grateful you're here now. The thought of tackling this on my own was pretty terrifying," Gran sniffed, pinching the bridge of her nose. "Your granddad took care of the big things. Tea?"

They might occasionally talk about being upset, but being staunch was also a major factor in their DNA. They were tough, and they liked it that way.

Gran's daughter, aka Maddie's mom, had been a handful, according to Gran. Ava Flynn broke both their hearts when she left, even though they'd tried every way they could think of to show her they loved her. It had gnawed at the young Maddie, and she knew it had affected Gran because she would sometimes catch her staring at a photo of Granddad and Mom.

Fifteen years later, Maddie's mother was still missed, but they had moved on from being sad, and tea was still the magic potion for everything. Being an Anglophile, anything English was close to Gran's heart, but tea was her main legacy from her parents. Born and raised in Liverpool, they had emigrated to America when Gran was a teenager, but she'd never forgotten her roots.

Her kitchen had shelves filled with an assortment of bric-a-brac that all in some way represented England. Single sets of matching cups and saucers with side plates, tea canisters with pictures of the royal family adorning them, and many teapots in a similar vein were lovingly dusted on a regular basis.

"I'd love a cup," Maddie said. "In fact, I need one. The traffic was horrible until we got past Portland. I hope one day they build an airport in Oregon closer to Maple Falls that's big enough to handle passenger planes." The one in Destiny was for light planes and helicopters, all privately owned.

Gran carefully took two cups and saucers from the shelf, along with side plates, while Maddie filled the kettle. It was an old relic passed down by Gran's mother, who had died long before Maddie was born and had instilled in her daughter the art of tea-making. Each set of cups and saucers was different and often had not been purchased together.

Over time, Gran had accumulated more than a dozen sets. If a person came for tea more than a couple of times, a particular set became theirs. Maddie always used the one with a pink rose, while Gran's favorite had lilacs.

"I haven't been to Portland since you were last home. Actually, it doesn't interest me to go far these days."

Maddie was plugging in the electric kettle that was as important as the best brand of tea that Gran insisted on using. She turned quickly. "You'd tell me if you were still unwell, wouldn't you?"

"Of course I would. Why do you ask?"

"You've always loved your weekly jaunts to anywhere the buses or trains would take you, and you've said more than once that you'd have to be taken out of this house in a coffin to get you to leave."

Gran laughed. "I did say that, didn't I? But things change, and I have to be realistic. I'm no longer a spring chicken. I'm also thinking about handing over the leadership of the community group to some younger blood."

"What? No way. Those ladies depend on you to liven things up around here." The club had been founded by Gran and a couple of her best friends, and they were forever searching for places to go and speakers who loved interesting things.

"That's the thing," Gran said. "They need to change it up. This is the twenty-first century, for goodness' sake. There must be other things to do that I've never heard of."

Maddie snorted at the idea of that group of women "changing things up". They were the happiest bunch of older men and women, doing what they loved, but perhaps not all as open to change as Gran.

Still, the club had played a big part in Gran's life, especially after Maddie left. Since Gran had never learned to drive, a bus or taxi was the only way for her to get around unless someone offered her a ride to Destiny. Every month, she organized the community group jaunt to somewhere as a day trip, as well as their speakers. It was a shock for Maddie to hear her giving up on it. Who would take that task on now?

Gran liked to be busy, and she also walked for miles. At least, she always had. She looked so healthy and fit, Maddie had a hard time thinking of her as either old or sickly.

"It's been good for me to be the president for so long, and it was something to keep me busy while you were away, but I'm over it," Gran continued. "I've been everywhere several dozen times, and now I can honestly say that staying around home is far more appealing."

"Except you're moving."

"That's true, but a home is whom you fill it with, not wood and nails."

Maddie's eyes prickled with tears, and she felt a distinct twinge of regret at the idea of someone else living here. Still, this was Gran's decision, not hers. She sucked up her sadness and smiled as she warmed the teapot and added English Breakfast tea leaves, their favorite, then filled it with boiling water.

"It's so nice to be back in Maple Falls and out of the rat race, but I only have a week, which means we need to get on to finding you a new place, pronto."

They sat at the old oak table, which had been scrubbed so often that it was now much paler than it had started out. Gran pushed a pile of brochures and papers at Maddie, as well as a large slice of pie. It was still warm, and Maddie took a forkful, then closed her eyes.

"Mmmm. I've missed your baking."

"I'm sure that after all that training in a French patisserie, yours is just as good, if not better."

Maddie tilted her head, savoring the pie. "Not quite. But it's getting close."

Honesty had been a strong part of growing up with Gran, who couldn't abide lies, so there was no point in false modesty. But how could you compare your own food with that of the woman whose recipes were loved by so many, and from whom you had begun to learn your craft? Gran had founded and fueled Maddie's passion for baking, a passion that had never waned.

She took another bite of pie. Yep, this was heaven on a plate. Gran was sitting across from her, patiently waiting for a decent pause, or for her to finish, whichever came first. Reluctantly, she put down her fork and spread out the brochures. Selling the family home was the right thing to do, but that didn't make it easier. These walls held so many memories—most of them happy.

Her heart sank at the sight of so many places to view. "Do you want to see all of these?"

"I've circled a few that may be of interest, but I wanted to discuss another option."

Maddie knew that tone. Gran could be very persuasive in general, but when she adopted that tone, you could bet something you weren't ready for was about to hit you squarely in the face and would probably stick like strawberry jam.

She took a few sips of the strong brew then a deep breath. "Okay. I'm ready. Tell me what you're up to."

Gran grimaced. "You're being a little dramatic, and it's not like I'd force anything on you."

She completely ignored Maddie's open mouth at the unfamiliar censure and tapped the top brochure.

"Here's the retirement community Angel took me to visit. It's quite nice, but they have a 'no overnight guests' policy, meaning you couldn't stay with me. I don't like that idea one bit." She turned it over and replaced it with several more. "There are these."

She flicked each one by Maddie's nose. Very fast. Maddie waited for the bomb to drop, and fortunately she only had to suffer the blur of papers for another few seconds.

"Then there's this. Now, I know you have your own plans, but please don't say no right away. Read it, go see it, then decide. Okay?"

Gran had begun to look jittery as she waved the paper in front of Maddie.

"Good gravy. How bad can this be? My nerves are turning to custard."

The slightly wrinkled chin lifted defiantly. "It's not bad at all. In fact, it's a wonderful opportunity if you can see the potential like I do."

Maddie pulled the paper from her hand so quickly that a small corner of it remained in Gran's fingertips. The front of the brochure was graced with a picture of a familiar block of four stores. A red rectangle was around one of them—the one Maddie noticed looked unkempt. At the end of the block, it not only sat on the main street of Maple Lane but backed onto Plum Place. Just up the road.

"I don't understand. You've decided to sell the house because it's too much. Why would you want a shop?"

Gran's eyebrows shot up. "For a bakery, of course. If I buy the shop, that one there"—she pointed at the red one— "it comes with a two-bedroom apartment upstairs, and since they all back onto our road, they have small yards of their own. It's a bit tired, but we've redecorated this house, so I know we can do the same to the shop and the apartment to make it just as lovely."

Maddie shut her gaping mouth with a snap. "You're not making sense. You can't manage a shop!"

Gran looked astounded, as if Maddie had stupidly missed the point. But what, exactly, *was* the point?

"No, I couldn't, but you could."

"Me?" Maddie was as confused as confectioners' sugar pretending to be frosting.

"For goodness' sake. I'm not speaking a foreign language. Isn't that your dream? To open your own bakery?"

Still feeling as if she were in an alternate universe, Maddie nodded. "Sure, but not here."

Gran sniffed. "Why not? I'd have thought Maple Lane was a perfect location."

Maddie had no idea what had brought on this weird conversation, but she wasn't liking where it was going. "It would be if I didn't plan on opening a bakery in New York City someday soon."

"It would be much cheaper to open one here."

Maddie tried to keep the frustration out of her voice. "That's true, but I don't have the money yet to buy a shop outright."

"Don't get prickly. I appreciate all of that. First, the owner is desperate to sell, so it's going for a song. Second, what if I put money in? I have savings. Or I could buy the whole thing outright with the sale from this place, and you could pay me back when you can."

Maddie was stunned for a moment. "No, Gran, I'm not taking your money. You've done so much for me already."

"I've done what family does when they love each other, nothing more. Anyway, you know everything I have will come to you when I'm pushing up daisies."

Maddie knew Gran wanted her back home, but this talk of not being around was scary, and it made her think once more that Gran might be sick and not telling her.

"You're not putting all your money into something that has no guarantee of success. I'll come home if you need me, but I'm not buying a shop in Maple Falls."

Gran looked down for a moment. When she raised her head, she tried to smile but failed miserably. "I totally understand. You should follow your heart and do what's right for you. Let's not talk about it anymore today. We can discuss more options tomorrow. Maybe I should rethink the retirement community."

Minutes ago, Gran had been excited about the prospect of going into business together, and now she looked utterly despondent. Was Maddie the worst granddaughter ever? She sure felt like it. Each bite turned to sawdust in her mouth.

This wasn't a good start. If Gran had her heart set on the business and the apartment, then one week would never be enough to talk her into something else. Clearly it couldn't be the retirement community if even the thought of it made her miserable.

A germ of an idea took hold, and Maddie grasped it with both hands. The shops had been there for decades, and the one Gran was talking about looked truly awful from the outside. The inside had to be as bad. Probably worse. Maybe if they took a look at it and Gran saw how much they'd have to do to get it up and running, she would change her mind.

Pleased with that idea and hopeful that they could find a nice place for Gran afterwards, she smiled. "On second thought, if you think it's worth our time, let's go see this place. After all, a look can't hurt, can it?"

Gran's face lit up once more. "Really? Now?"

Maddie raised an eyebrow. "Maybe I could finish my tea and pie?"

Gran leaned back with an air of satisfaction. "Take as long as you like. I'll give the agent a call in a minute. Should I say to meet her there in half an hour?"

Maddie spluttered her mouthful of tea over the pristine white tablecloth. She had the feeling that she'd just been played, but she couldn't think of anything to say in the face of such eagerness. She dabbed at the mess with a napkin while Gran brought the phone to the table.

She'd never made Maddie feel anything but wanted and loved, and doing anything to make Gran happy had never been an issue. Unfortunately, this felt like a step too far.

As soon as her plate was empty, Gran dialed the number and it was then that Maddie realized whom she was calling. They both knew the owner of the local real estate business, and the thought of seeing Virginia Bolton, let alone discussing business with her, was enough to make Maddie's insides turn to jelly.

What a morning, and it wasn't done yet.

. . .

Need more? Pick up Apple Pie and Arsenic here!

Don't forget to sign up for my new release mailing list and pick up a free recipe book. I promise not to spam you.

And, if you loved Mocha Mayhem, I'd very much appreciate a review. :-)

RECIPES

These recipes are ones I use all the time and have come down the generations from my mum, grandmother, and some I have adapted from other recipes.

Also, I am now in possession of my husband's grandmother's recipe book. Exciting! I'll be bringing some of them to life very soon.

Just a wee reminder that I am a New Zealander. Occasionally, I may have missed converting into ounces and pounds for my American readers.

My apologies for that, and please let me know if you do try them, how they turn out.

Keep well.
Cheryl x

MOCHA CUPCAKES

I ngredients:
  2 tbsp instant coffee
  1 ¼ cups / 150 g self-raising flour
  1 ¾ cup / 165 g soft light brown sugar
  6 oz butter or margarine
  3 medium eggs
  ¼ Tblsp milk
  Pinch of salt

Instructions:

1. Pre-heat your oven to 160ºC/140ºC fan.

2. Place your cupcake cases into a muffin tin.

3. Sift the self-raising flour, coffee powder and salt into the bowl of your mixer. Add the eggs, butter or margarine, brown sugar, and milk. Mix on slow speed until fully combined.

4. Half fill the muffin cases with the mixture. An ice-cream scoop is perfect for this.

5. Bake for 18-20 minutes until a skewer inserted into the

middle comes out clean. Leave the cupcakes to cool in their tins for about 10 minutes and then move them to a wire rack to cool fully before decorating.

Mocha Frosting

Ingredients:
1 ¼ cup or butter or margarine
3 ½ cups icing sugar
¼ tsp vanilla extract
3 tbsp instant coffee
1 ½ tbsp boiling water

Instructions:
1. Mix the instant coffee granules with the boiling water. Set aside to cool.

2. Beat the butter or margarine until with an electric mixer. Add the icing / confectioners sugar a little at a time and beat until fully combined.

3. Add the vanilla extract and the cooled coffee and mix.

4. The consistency should be soft yet firm.

5. Place mocha cream in your piping bag and frost your cakes by starting from the outside and moving in a continuous circle finishing in the middle.

Tip: If the frosting is too stiff, beat in a little milk.

BOOKS BY CHERYL PHIPPS

Sycamore Springs Series

The Trouble with Friends

The Trouble with Exes

The Trouble with Love

Dreamers Bay Series - Set in New Zealand

Dreamers Bay Series – Books 1-4

One More Chance

One More Kiss

One More Dance

One More Step

Billionaire Knights Series

Billionaire Knights Books 1-5

Restless Billionaire

Ruthless Billionaire

Reluctant Billionaire

Reckless Billionaire

Resident Billionaire

Millionaire - Family Ties Series

The Millionaire Next Door

The Millionaire's Proposal

The Millionaire's Seduction

High Seas Weddings

Against the Tide

Waves of Passion

Kisses on the Sand - Coming soon!

Romantic Suspense

When We Break

Please note: most of these are available in paperback.

ABOUT THE AUTHOR

C. A. Phipps is a USA Today Bestselling Author.

'Life is a mystery.'

Cheryl loves a good mystery filled with feisty heroines and wonderful small towns with heart-warming tales of strong family ties mixed in with a little romance and humor.

She lives in a quiet suburb of New Zealand's largest city, Auckland, with her wonderful husband, who she married the moment she left school (yes, they were high school sweethearts).

A lover of animals, with a few children, and even more grandchildren, who keep her young, she loves family times, dining out, baking and travel.

www.caphipps.com
cherylphippsbooks@gmail.com

Made in the USA
Monee, IL
27 April 2022

95530042R00148